HIDDEN PATHS

DANIEL ROLPH

To every child who has endured trauma.
Your strength, your story, and your journey matter. This is for you and
the resilience you carry with you each and every day.

FOREWORD

Hidden Paths is not just a story—it's a reflection of my life growing up in the UK care system. As a child, I experienced the highs and lows of foster care, and these books are my way of giving a voice to those children who, like me, felt invisible and unheard.

However, Hidden Paths is more than a tale of foster care. It's a story about resilience, identity, and survival—universal themes that resonate with anyone who has faced hardship. While the focus may be on childhood trauma, rejection, and the fight to belong, I believe that most of us, at some point in our lives, have navigated our own challenges.

Through these stories, I aim not only to shed light on the often-overlooked realities of foster care and childhood trauma but also to connect with anyone who has ever felt lost, rejected, or misunderstood. My hope is to encourage reflection and start conversations about the inner strength that carries us through life's hardest moments.

HIDDEN PATHS

CHAPTER 1

After finishing the first book in this series, I sometimes wondered about how you, the reader, would feel reading about the other two people who shared so much of my life during those difficult years in the system. You have, after all, already shared so much about Emma and Ollie's lives just by reading about them in my own story, and yet there is still so much more for you to discover.

If you think that the three of us ended up living the best lives imaginable, then you are sadly mistaken. Like I said before, real life rarely offers fairy tale endings. I think that's why we make up stories in the first place, to hide the harsh reality of life from ourselves. If I had to choose the hardest of our three lives to share, it might surprise you to learn that I wouldn't choose me at all, or Ollie, for that matter. I think Emma is the one who faced the worst of it, and it was because of the letters and long-distance conversations we shared during subsequent years that I found the truth behind her smile.

Before compiling all of the different notes and letters into the following story, I thought I knew my friend well enough to understand her background. She'd opened up to me many times before the day she asked me to share her story, and once I agreed, I found an entirely different person before me. A new level of gloom consumed the facade she'd put up for most of her life. I say a facade because it takes a special kind of person to be able to hide the type of trauma she endured, not just during her later years when sitting in the middle of maximum security, but also during those early years when we would spend time together playing Mario Kart in my room back at Kay and Roger's home.

I shudder to think of what nightmares she must have carried around with her, some hiding right behind that smile of hers, the one she'd put on whenever close to people she really cared about. It was her way of protecting us, I think, not that she ever came right out and admitted so. That I had to guess for myself, thanks to the multitude of conversations we had in the prison visit rooms.

If it surprises you to learn that Emma ended up in prison like Ollie, then I've got news for you. Her story goes into much darker territory, darker than even some of my worst experiences. It took us many attempts to try and get the whole story out, as each time we tried, the emotional scars became too much for her to bear, and we had to revisit them at a later date. I spent more time sitting in prison waiting rooms trying to get inside to see her than actually being with her. If you've never been to a jail yourself and experienced trying to get inside, then picture a medical facility's waiting room bursting with patients and half the staff missing.

The first time Emma ended up in jail was in March of 2005, just a few years after she first took that awful job in Paris. I say awful because I believe it might have been the one that ultimately sent her down the path to total self-destruction. Were it not for the isolation from her friends, she might have stood a chance to save herself, but unfortunately, it wasn't to be.

That was the first time she ever called me for help, *real* help. I remember the fear in her voice when I took the call, the kind of fear that sends genuine shivers down your spine. It was also the first time I ever heard Emma use the word beg when asking for something, as if doubting whether I was taking her seriously.

"Please, Jack, I beg you," she pleaded. "Please come and help me." It had been the guarded tone that really chilled me, as if she were trying to hide the call from someone.

I had been in the middle of detailing this new Jaguar that had just come in, a 1988 XJ6 model. Louis had asked me to take special care of it as he already had a potential buyer interested in it. Personally, I'm not much of a Jaguar guy, especially that one which came in this gaudy green colour. Give me a Mustang any day.

The second I heard the phone ringing in my pocket, I knew it was her. I mean, I knew even before checking the screen for the Caller ID. I don't know if there was some sort of telepathic connection between us or what, but I just knew it was Emma and that she was in trouble. The second I answered the call, I heard it in her voice.

"I'm in trouble, Jack. Real trouble." I heard genuine panic, my own insides ramping up accordingly. "I need help. Please." She paused. I heard a kind of muffling sound before she came back; this time, her voice lowered considerably. "Please, Jack. I need your help."

"Em, slow down," I said, trying to calm her down but having very little effect.

"Jack, she's dead, holy shit, she's dead. I need -"

"Em, EM." I took a breath. "Please calm down and breathe." When she paused long enough for me to speak again, I calmed my voice and continued. "Tell me what happened."

This time when she spoke, her voice sounded a lot more controlled, although still prone to jittery outbursts of emotion. I got the crux of the issue almost immediately. Emma and her friend, Melanie, had gone to a party with another friend of theirs, and this friend brought some pills with her. At some point, she asked Emma to hold them, and because of she getting a little too caught up in the fun, she forgot about them sitting in her handbag. At some point through the night, the friend collapsed, and despite attempts by paramedics to resuscitate her, she died in the ambulance on the way to the hospital. Somehow, Emma ended up being interviewed by the police, and when they checked her handbag, they found the stash of pills.

Along with a possession charge, she had also been charged with manslaughter, although the prosecutor was hunting around for even more. Add to that the fact that Emma had turned eighteen just a couple of months earlier, and she was now classed as an adult, and adults served jail time in adult jails. The only good thing we had on our side, as far as I knew, was that the party had been held in London, not Paris, where the girls had been working. That meant Emma was being held on our side of the Channel.

I did finish detailing the Jaguar as best I could, but I immediately asked to leave the second I finished it. After a quick taxi ride to the police station, I sat in the waiting room, hoping to have a chance to speak with her, but of course, it wasn't allowed. The policeman manning the front desk barely acknowledged my request. It was only by sheer luck that I heard him answer a woman's question about Emma Grant that I knew she was her barrister.

"I'm Jack Hardy," I said to her when she, too, was directed to take a seat in the waiting room. "I heard you mention my friend, Emma Grant?"

"You know Emma?" I nodded.

"I'm guessing this isn't something that's going to get resolved today?" She surprised me with her response.

"Possibly, if I can get in to see her soon."

She introduced herself as Kelly Mann, and while she wasn't able to get Emma out of jail that day, she did manage it the following day, courtesy of an early afternoon bail hearing. I sat in and listened, no easy thing when watching one of your closest friends close to breaking point. Emma looked a frightful mess, her face screwed into mass panic as the fear ravaged her. I could see from where I was sitting that she was visibly shaking the entire time, her fingers trembling as they tried to wrestle each other for control.

When the judge eventually granted bail, I had hoped to see

some of the stress vanish from Emma's face, but it didn't. She looked just as unhinged an hour later when she walked out of the courthouse beside her barrister. The second she saw me, she ran over and flung her arms around my neck before breaking down and crying. I could barely support her and had to follow her down to the concrete, where we took a moment for her to regain control.

For the next month, Emma stayed with me in the granny flat, trying to prepare herself for the possibility of doing jail time. Her barrister warned her that the case against her looked solid, and unless they could prove some mitigating circumstances, she would more than likely lose. We spoke about it at length almost every night after I came home from work, sometimes staying up until the early hours of the morning, but no matter how much I tried to reassure her that it would be OK, she didn't believe me. Sometimes, Ollie would also come over and try to talk her down, but even his advice didn't help.

Eventually, her hunch proved correct, and Emma ended up with a four-year sentence for involuntary manslaughter, a non-parole period of two. She broke down as the judge read the sentence out and had to be helped by court security. I still feel the chills run through me thinking about it, remembering the scream she let out at the moment of sentencing. A raw explosion of deep-seated fear tore from her throat and echoed across the courtroom. Beside me, Ollie physically jumped.

While we all assumed that the case had been the worst part, the real nightmare was about to begin. After already suffering through nearly every form of punishment possible, Emma was about to enter a new kind of torture, the kind she would be unable to escape from. It was only because of our subsequent talks and exchanges that I eventually found out about the real happenings behind the wall.

The words you are about to read are those from Emma herself, rewritten by me in a way that makes them a little easier to comprehend. She tried so very hard to give us an honest look into the life of a girl who entered the system as a damaged four-year-old and ultimately fell to the pressures her world forced upon her. It is a story steeped in the kind of trauma hidden behind closed doors, whispered about in dark alleys, and rarely acknowledged. And for me, it is also one of the most tragic stories of all.

CHAPTER 2

Scrawny. That was the initial thought that came to my mind the first time I ever set eyes on Jack. He'd been walking around the perimeter of the park and pretending not to notice me. Our eyes would randomly meet at different points in his walk as he would momentarily disappear behind a tree or piece of play equipment before reappearing and looking in my direction. I could feel my cheeks heat up each time we spotted each other, another unwanted reminder of not only my shyness, but also that fear of being called out as a member of the rag brigade.

The thing is, there was something about the boy I couldn't ignore, an unseen connection somehow bringing us together. Perhaps it had been fate's intention all along for us to meet that morning, each of us making a series of choices that would ultimately converge our paths into a single point. Maybe it was just the familiarity I could sense, that underlying primal understanding of recognising one of my own. Or, dramatics aside, it could have been nothing more than my over-imaginative brain trying to give me validation, and Jack was nothing more than an unexpected blip on my radar that day. Whatever it was, it brought us together and ultimately changed both our lives forever.

In a weird kind of way, I think it was Ollie who was always meant to complete our little circle of friends, despite my meeting him before Jack. It was only after the latter came along that the three of us became this package deal, in a way, but it was with Jack that I always had a much closer bond, despite what others might tell you.

I still believe that my meeting with Ollie happened completely by chance, although some might tell you differently. They'll go into great detail about how the universe has this complete plan for everybody, even unwanted rag brigade members like me, and every decision we make is just part of that plan. I guess, in a way, it could be right, given that Henry Fawkner was about as predictable as a rabid dog.

I'd arrived at the Fawkner home a month earlier, and while Louise, the wife and mother of the six-year-old twins, did welcome me with open arms, it was her husband, Henry, whom I couldn't bring myself to trust from the first moment I laid eyes on him.

Henry had this kind of stare, one that didn't stop with just my face. His eyes had a way of working their way down the length of my body, briefly pausing at the newly developed bumps I still couldn't recognise as being a permanent part of me. His stare almost went *through* my clothes, feeling almost as invasive as if he'd been using his hands instead of his eyes to do the exploring for him. It was because of that discomfort that I started locking the door to my bedroom almost immediately, something Louise didn't discover for almost three months.

Jack and I shared many talks together over the years, and I think he was one of the few people in my life who genuinely understood what it meant to survive the system we had ended up falling into. While Ollie did as well, he was one of the few people I knew who tried to *bury* the truth instead, almost running from reality, which is what I think eventually caught up with him during the darkest times. Not Jack. You could look him in the eyes and see the scarred soul wearing those experiences like body armour.

I guess, if I'm going to be telling you about survival, then I should probably start from the very beginning, the place where my world took a dark and sinister turn and forever changed the course of my life. It is the story of how each event took me on a journey through some of my darkest days before I eventually ended up in one of the most inhumane places imaginable.

The thing about my story, my *real* story, is that it might not surprise you at all, at least not in the beginning. It is, perhaps, one of those tales with a very predictable beginning, the circumstances so similar to many of those who shared the rag brigade tag. My mother had me when she was just a child herself, the birth occurring three days before her sixteenth birthday. And while she did try to raise me herself, the pressure from others became too much for her, and I was put up for adoption within just four months of coming into this world.

Yes, I guess I could be angry with her for the lack of planning on her part. Should she have used protection in that brief moment of lust when my father, a twenty-seven-year-old unemployed drug addict from Braunstone, Leicester, managed to convince her that he was the best choice at that moment? Maybe.

Their courtship could be described as a pretty classic scenario, given the way it played out. They met at a party, got drunk, and nine months later, I emerged into a broken family where all seven of my mother's siblings lived on the dole and scrounging off the system. Oh, and in case you're wondering, my maternal grandmother hasn't held a steady job since 1985, having given birth to the first of eight early that year.

The thing is, my mum wanted to be different. She could have kept me, of course, and claimed money off the system the way the rest of her family had been doing for years, but I think shame is what drove her to try and follow her dreams, dreams which eventually led her to London. That was where she met Roger Holmes, a handsome thirty-year-old who first got her addicted to heroin and then forced her into prostitution, where her second client strangled my mum in his car before dumping her body into the Thames.

I didn't find out about my mum until years later, of course, and

I'll share more of that side of things later. Right now, I need you to know that my first seven years of life began in the home of another family, one that took care of me the way any regular family would have. It's not like I had anything to compare them to, and so it just felt normal. Looking back now, it's more than obvious that it wasn't exactly a warm and loving home, but Peggy and Brian never mistreated me. I probably could have remained with them for my entire childhood, were it not for my adopted father passing away from a stroke while driving his taxi. That one event set the wheels in motion for the bank to repossess the family home, and me being sent to an orphanage after Peggy broke down from the grief and stress, eventually ending up in a home needing twenty-four-seven care.

And that is where this story truly begins for me, the day a smartly dressed woman came to the house, helped me pack a suitcase, and then drove me the forty minutes down the road to an ominous building that I was supposed to call home.

"But I don't want to leave," I told the woman when she initially pulled a much too large suitcase from the top of the wardrobe and carried it into my room. I remember looking around for Peggy, but she had vanished in the blink of an eye, the house feeling unusually empty for the first time in my life.

"There's nothing for you here now, child," the woman who had introduced herself as Claudette said to me. Back then, her tone had a certain finality about it, but thinking back now, I wonder how anybody could expect a seven-year-old child to understand the meaning of having no choice.

St. Agnes Home for Girls. That's where Claudette took me that fateful morning, an event that has been permanently etched into my memory. I still remember the chill from the drizzle hitting my face as we walked towards the building's front doors, with the thick blanket of clouds hanging low and heavy only adding to the misery. I stopped at one point to look up into the sky with my eyes closed, figuring that if I was going to get wet, then I might as well do a proper job of it. I remember my eye sockets filling up with cold water that ran down my face when Claudette pushed me along with impatient hands.

"You'll catch a chill," she said as I struggled to catch my feet, her push almost sending me face-first into the concrete path. Her words sounded panicked, as if she hadn't expected to send me stumbling and wanted to excuse her action.

Once inside, the ambience didn't get any better, with the same dreariness of the outside world continuing in the foyer. The walls, painted a light grey pastel, appeared old and faded, a visual marker adding to the damp smell of the foyer. The fake black-and-white chequered tiles on the linoleum floors had probably been freshly laid several decades earlier, with countless boots and shoes wearing them out over the years.

"Ah, Mrs. Murphy," a voice called from the top of the staircase, and when I looked up, I saw a nun standing at the very top, her hands clasped in front of her as she slowly began to descend the stairs.

The first time I met Sister Celia, she barely paid me the slightest attention as she greeted Claudette with nothing more than a stern look and a nod in the direction of an open office door. She did gaze down at me over the top of her thin gold glasses with a frown as she walked past me, but stopped short of actually acknowledging my presence.

"I was expecting you an hour ago," the nun said when she walked into her office and sat behind the desk.

"My apologies, Sister," Claudette said. "The morning traffic got the -"

"Never mind about that now, the nun said as she sifted through a bunch of files on her desk, pulled one free, and opened it up to reveal two slips of paper, one of which she held out to Claudette. "Usual signatures on there," she said, turning her attention to the other, which she began to write on.

As for me? I stood there like an unwanted pet, feeling completely out of place and more uncomfortable than I had ever felt in my short life. I looked around the office not because of intrigue, but rather to give myself purpose. I thought that if I tried to get a clearer idea of where I was, then maybe it would suppress that awful feeling of abandonment.

Abandonment. How does society explain the meaning of such a word to a four-year-old in a way that she can clearly understand? That's how old I was when Peggy and Brian told me I had been adopted because my real mother had abandoned me. That word, that…confusingly dark word, ran through my brain for countless nights those first few years, as if tormenting me from the shadows of my mind. I had actually thought that it had left me for good, at one point, but when it came back while I stood in that office watching the nun writing on that slip of paper, I wondered whether that was the word fate had allocated to me for life.

Granted, I had a few years already to consider its true meaning, but nothing will ever feel more disheartening than standing in the middle of an office surrounded by people who feel nothing but frustration by your very presence. The word only confused me when I first heard it at four years old, but feeling it at seven? That's a brutal introduction to a new way of life.

I was sure that St. Agnes Home for Girls was the kind of place I'd seen in a couple of movies over the preceding years. You know the kind where the lonely protagonist gets sent to an orphanage, where she falls under the control of a ruthless antagonist, and eventually escapes into the world where she finds a miracle family who ends up adopting her. Annie, anyone? Is that one of them? I can't remember, having blocked most of them from my mind for obvious reasons. In my world, and the world of many abandoned children such as myself, miracles rarely come our way; our lives are stuck in a perpetual loop of misery and isolation.

I must have stood uncomfortably in that office for close to ten minutes while the two women continued to fill out the necessary paperwork for my transfer. Forget about small talk. Sister Celia didn't strike me as the kind of woman who mingled with mere mortals. Not even as a lonely and frightened seven-year-old did I see a bright side to her. The woman's stern face appeared scrunched up in an endless frown, as if any task had been inter-rupted by some important task.

"Right, here you go," Sister Celia said when she set the pen down and held out her sheet of paper.

"Thank you," Claudette said, taking it and holding out her own.

Having exchanged forms and finishing their paperwork, both women stood. Claudette looked at me and knelt down to look at me on my level.

"You will have a wonderful home here, Emma," she said with a forced smile. "Sister Celia takes care of lots of girls your age, and I'm sure you'll make many friends."

"Yes, of course she will," the nun said, her tone making the words sound matter-of-factly.

I walked back out into the foyer behind Claudette and watched her leave via the front door, never turning back to give me that final farewell wave you always see in the movies. It was as if she finished her job with those final few words of encouragement and now turned her attention to whatever came next. I never saw her again, not directly anyway. There was that one time I watched her walking away from the building, but that is one time I'd rather forget. And while her leaving me standing in that home effectively closed the woman's chapter in my story, a new one had just begun.

CHAPTER 3

Sarah Louise Clayton. That was the name of the first friend I ever made at St. Agnes, a girl I met shortly after arriving. The transition from the foyer of the building to the second-floor dormitory took less than a minute once Sister Celia beckoned for me to follow her. The nun only frowned when it looked like I might start crying from the confusion and fear, and she completely ignored my suitcase that she walked past on her way to the stairs. Forcing the tears back, I grabbed the handle of the suitcase and trudged up those stairs, promising myself not to show weakness to the woman.

"Bathroom is the last door on the left," Sister Celia said when we reached the second-floor corridor, before pointing to a closer door. "That's where your floor monitor, Sister Alice, resides." I had no idea what a floor monitor was, of course, and so had no idea what to do with the information. "And this is where you'll be staying."

We walked into a room filled with bunks, maybe four or five sets. A couple of girls sitting on top of one looked over at us, their expressions both curious and contemptuous. One of them tapped the other's leg, and when they exchanged a glance, it was obvious what they thought.

"Sarah," Sister Celia called out towards another girl sitting alone on one of the bottom bunks. The girl looked up from the book she was reading.

"Yes?"

"Don't yes me, girl. You come when summoned," the nun snapped with authority.

"Yes, Sister," the girl said and quickly slid off the bed. The other two sitting on top of the bunk smirked, one of them letting a slight giggle out. When the nun looked in their direction, the giggling girl immediately lost her grin and cast her eyes down.

I could tell almost immediately that Sister Celia wasn't the kind of person a kid messed with. While I still hadn't seen the worst of her, the reactions from the other kids were enough of a warning for me.

"Sarah, I'd like you to show Emma how things work around here. She'll be taking the bunk above yours, so make sure she settles in and then report back to me."

"Yes, Sister," the girl said before the nun turned around and walked out, leaving me to fend for myself.

The first thing I heard was the girls on top of the bunk whispering something to each other, but making sure I could still hear them. They held their hands up to their mouths and kept their mouths hidden, taking animated glances in my direction.

"Hi, I'm Sarah," the girl standing next to me said. "Don't mind them, they tend to pick on every new person."

"I'm Emma," I said, and while I had an urge to shake hands as if needing to make it official like a grown-up, the girl turned around before I could offer it.

"Your bed is this way," she said and kept walking to the other side of the large room.

There were others in the room with us, but none who bothered to react to the new person's arrival. Some read books, others were colouring in, while one girl appeared to be sleeping on the floor under her bed. Sarah saw me watching her as we walked by.

"That's Hailey," she said. "You'll often find her lying under her bed. She spends more time there than actually on her bed."

"Why?" I asked.

"Who knows," Sarah said with a shrug of her shoulders. She stopped beside a set of bunks and pointed to the top one. "Well, that's you. There's a spare drawer in that cabinet over there, aaaaand you can keep your suitcase under the bunks."

At first, I felt like I had maybe fallen into a bad dream and didn't know how to wake up again. The room felt…hmm, how do I describe it without sounding too dramatic? It felt abrasive, in a way, not warm and welcoming, the way a home should. You have to remember that I came from a family that had not only adopted me, but also taken care of me the way decent parents would.

Most days, I barely remembered that I wasn't their natural offspring, which I wasn't made aware of until I was four years old. I guess my adopted parents wanted me to know from an early age, as they believed that the transition is so much easier the younger a person is. It just became a fact and not something to get upset over. I also barely remember life before knowing about it anyway. It's not as if I still had any memories from living with my actual mother, and none of that family ever bothered to visit. As far as I was concerned, Peggy and Brian were my parents, and that's all there was to it. That was until Brian suffered a stroke at the wheel of his taxi, and Peggy couldn't cope without him.

You must forgive me for the lack of information about the time I spent with Peggy and Brian, but the truth is that I want to keep that part of my life private. It changes nothing about the rest of my story and has little significance when it comes to the brutal system I ended up in. My first ever foster parents never did anything wrong by me. I loved them, respected them, and accepted that they did the best they could for the time they had. In a way, I think it was a fair trade-off, with me giving them the years of helping them believe they had a child of their own. I guess I needed them just as much as they needed me.

That first moment after arriving at St. Agnes felt like I had been physically torn from the only home I had ever known and thrown into a prison with other kids who also had no parents. We were outcasts, rejected by those who could have made a difference and forced to live in a place designed to be as miserable as possible. Why do I think that they tried to make the home as miserable as possible?

"So that when you do end up in a house with new parents, you won't expect too much," was how Sarah described it later that afternoon when we were sitting on her bunk getting to know one another.

"How long have you been here?" I asked her after thinking about her answer.

"About fourteen months now. I arrived on my seventh birthday, if you can believe that."

"Did they at least throw you a party?" Sarah chuckled, but tried to keep the noise just between the two of us.

"A party? Seriously?" She shook her head. "Sometimes, we have a cake for people's birthdays, but not all the time. It just depends on who is in the kitchen on the day."

"What do you mean?"

"Well, Old Bill isn't prone to baking cakes for birthdays, but Deloris does the occasional sponge. They take turns cooking for us," Sarah said, and just as I was about to ask why, the bunk bed suddenly shook violently before a head suddenly hung down over the edge of the top bunk.

"Deloris is my favourite," the new upside-down face said with a grin.

"Same," Sarah said, then added, "Emma, this is Gracie. She's on the top bunk next to yours." As I was about to say hi, Sarah whispered, "Careful, because she snores."

"I do not," the new girl said and swung a leg around before dropping to the ground with a loud thud.

"She does," Sarah whispered before Gracie playfully slapped her leg.

"Don't make me beat you," she said with a giggle before running off again.

"She's actually hyper," Sarah said once we were alone again. "That's what Sister Alice calls it."

I looked around for a moment, listening to the sounds of a room I now had to call home. There wasn't much to see, just four walls, five bunk beds arranged in a neat row, a tiny play area where used toys sat neatly arranged into two wooden crates, a crucifix hanging on one wall, and a painting of Jesus surrounded by his disciples on the opposite wall. As for the ambient sounds, those came more from the rooms and floors both above and below us. Most I still couldn't identify, but I did recognize Sister Celia's voice calling out for someone to hurry up with the mop.

The room I had been assigned to was one of four, with two on our floor and another two on the building's third floor. There were about forty girls in total, although Sarah said that this number fluctuated from one week to the next, depending on how many cycled in and out. Those living on the floor above ours were aged ten to fifteen, while those on my floor were all under ten, with the youngest just two.

Sister Alice came to welcome me to the floor just before dinner that first day, and I could tell right away that she would be the one I'd connect with the most. I'm not sure how old she was, but I do know that she must have been considerably younger than Sister Celia, just based on her appearance alone. Even as a seven-year-old, I could tell that she displayed far fewer wrinkles, which Sarah said was because the woman didn't frown anywhere near as much as Sister Celia.

The other thing I liked about Sister Alice was that she seemed like she had a genuine interest in me. She asked questions right from the start, not just about how I was settling in and whether I had made any friends yet, but also about who I was and where I came from. She held my eyes, looking at me without distraction, the way so many grown-ups did as I answered each of her questions. We had genuine conversations, if that makes sense.

It was Sister Alice who ended up giving me a proper tour of the home, with Sarah coming along for good measure. I think Sister Alice preferred someone else to tag along, as it helped ease my nerves. She showed me the third-floor bedrooms, introduced me to a few of the older girls, and even let me watch them playing a game of Monopoly that she said the girls had been playing for four days straight.

When we walked into the dining room, I saw several rows of tables and chairs filling the middle, while a hole in one of the walls looked directly into the kitchen, where a single chef worked a cooker of some sort. Two of the older girls stood near the serving station and were busy dishing out meals as the rest of the kids lined up with plates in hand.

"It's lasagna night," Sister Alice whispered in my ear as she held an empty plate out to me and grabbed one for herself. She gestured for me to stand ahead in line and then stood behind me. "It's my favourite as it means Deloris has also made her chocolate pudding for sweets."

"Is it nice?" I asked, and Sister Alice rolled her eyes, her lips tight as she tried to hide the grin.

"To die for," she whispered back. "Honestly."

The kids didn't start eating when they sat down at the tables. Instead, they all seemed to wait for the rest of the group to be served their meal and take their seats. Once the servers had cleared the line and brought their own plates to the table, Sister Alice began the prayer while everyone else linked hands. What's weird is that while I had never prayed before, I sat between Sarah and another girl, feeling somewhat normal for the first time that day. Yes, normal. It was as if that small bit of human contact, sharing a moment of connection, was somehow enough to ease my mind and make me believe that I truly belonged. If only the rest of my time at the home could have felt the same.

CHAPTER 4

There are a few moments in my life that feel like markers, moments in time that I distinctly remember, and perhaps serve as permanent memories. Sitting here while writing this, I try to remember some random moments from my time at St. Agnes, from mundane mealtimes to some Saturday afternoons spent watching movies in the rec room.

The most vivid memory I probably have is that first night lying awake in bed. Sister Alice had switched off the lights about an hour before, after making her rounds. With around twenty kids spread across two rooms to look after, she didn't rush through the place, instead taking her time to interact with everybody. She even stood beside my bunk, asking whether I was OK to have the lights out and if the dark bothered me. I lied, of course. Show me a seven year-old not afraid of the monsters hiding in the shadows.

It wasn't until the lights were actually switched off that the harsh reality, my *new* reality, really hit home. I was alone, though not alone, surrounded by more kids than I could have imagined, and yet felt more distant than ever. The thing that probably confused me the most was that I missed a woman I had no memories of, a woman who had been dead for years, and yet still hung onto such a large portion of my heart.

Did I cry that first night at St. Agnes? Yes, I did. No shame there. Any kid my age would have, maybe even those older than me. But my tears weren't for me, or for Peggy and Brian. My tears were for my mother, the woman with whom I should have been living life. We should have been in some house, with a dog and a cat. I should have had my own bedroom and a living room, and a kitchen table where we would eat our meals and catch up on whatever the day had brought us.

I didn't cry for a life lost but rather for a life that had never been, a life I only ever imagined for myself, and usually when I felt the most isolated. That first night, I didn't bury my face in the pillow and try to silence the sobbing because there was none. I lay on my side, the tears rolling silently down onto the pillow while I stared into the shadows of the room. The sounds of the others barely registered, the snores and the brief coughs blending into the background.

Sleep did eventually take me that night, and I distinctly remember floating down a river on a small boat with my mother. She looked so happy, the sunshine reflecting off the water and sending these glistening sparkles across her face. I could hear her laughing, pointing to something in the distance. And when I was about to get up from my seat and walk to her, a voice calling my name pulled me from the dream.

"Emma Grant, you will wake up this instant, young lady," Sister Celia called from the doorway.

My eyes sprang awake in an instant, and I jumped from the top bunk before I realized where I was. I hit the floor hard, felt something painful twist in my ankle, and collapsed to the ground with a burning sensation shooting up my leg. I cried out in pain and felt fresh tears coming on, and when nobody came to my aid, I realized I was the only kid still in the room.

"Now that was a silly thing to do, wasn't it?" Sister Celia said as she walked between two of the bunks.

At first, she didn't lean down to help me, instead watching me from her vantage point, perhaps considering whether I was worth the effort. The pain seemed to get worse, and when I tried to stand on the ankle, I just about fainted from the pain.

"No, no, stay there," Sister Celia said with animated frustration. She actually sighed loudly and shook her head as she turned away, as if my accident had somehow infringed on her day. "I'll find someone to help you."

Unbelievably, she left the room, leaving me alone for however long as I continued fighting the tears that sat right on the very edge. That wasn't how I wanted to spend the first day in my new home, not when first impressions mattered. This was the point in time when other kids would decide who I was, what name to call me, and what insecurities I had. This was when the bullies took notes and decided whether I was worth the effort.

As it turned out, a broken ankle didn't bring any bullies my way, or at least not that day. Instead, I ended up the centre of attention, the other kids all piling around me when I came back from the hospital wearing a new plaster cast around the bottom of my leg. It wasn't how I expected to spend the first day, but in a way, I think it ended up being something of a blessing. By the time dinner time rolled around, the cast looked like it had been set a week earlier, with almost every space filled with messages and signatures. Even Deloris, the cook, came and signed my cast during dinner, adding a little smiling sun sketch to her name.

My favourite time of the day was the two hours between the end of dinner and when we had to go to bed. The majority of kids spent the time in one of the two rec rooms, either watching television, playing video games, or playing board games. A few mainly kept to themselves, either sitting in a corner colouring in, or reading a book. Not me, and especially not that evening. I became the centre of attention, with some of the girls offering to do virtually anything for me. They fetched me glasses of water, fluffed a pillow behind my back, and one girl sat at my feet with my injured cast resting across her lap.

That night, I felt like nothing I had ever experienced before. It felt like the entire world had suddenly discovered who I was and came to befriend me. The kids offered to play Monopoly, put whatever movie I wanted to watch on the TV, and engaged in conversation. Unlike the world I had known before, this one threw me into the very middle like I was some kind of celebrity. If only it could have lasted.

Three days later, my life took another turn with the arrival of Lydia Nutworth, a twelve-year-old girl who had been living with a family for the previous year, prior to which she had lived in the very same bunk I now resided in. The second she walked into the rec room that Sunday afternoon, she made a beeline for me and immediately got in my face.

"I want my bed back," she snapped, foregoing any hint of a greeting. The others sitting on the nearby couch looked over as the room fell into silence. I'm not just talking about a few kids turning to see what was going on, but the entire space suddenly falling into complete silence as the crowd seemed to hold its breath in anticipation of what would come next.

"I-I don't think we're allowed to move," I said, remembering Sister Celia specifically telling someone else that bed placements were final after a couple of girls brought it up.

"I wasn't asking," the girl snarled. She leaned down to stare at me with her beady little eyes that I swear lacked any hint of colour. The devil himself couldn't have had blacker eyes, and I felt my insides tighten with fear.

"What's going on in here?"

I looked past the girl to see Sister Alice standing in the doorway, and when she spotted her, the expression went from mild curiosity to immediate understanding.

"Ah, Lydia, you're back," Sister Alice said.

"Yes, I am," the girl said, not bothering to look around. Instead, she kept the same threatening gaze on me that sent the hairs on the back of my neck upright.

"I believe Sister Celia assigned you to Room 2, Bunk 4A."

"I want my old bed back," Lydia snapped, still staring at me.

"Your old bed is occupied," Sister Alice said with a lot more conviction. "Nobody keeps their bed allocation once they leave, you know that."

"I don't care," Lydia said, looking around at the nun for the first time. "It's *my* bed."

"I beg to differ, and this isn't the place to be having this discussion."

"I'll get you for this," was what the girl whispered to me just before she turned and stormed from the room. Sister Alice gave me an empathic smile, but I somehow knew it wouldn't be enough to protect me.

I don't think I really needed someone else to tell me that I was about to find myself in a world of pain, but Sarah did take the time to point it out to me once Lydia had left the room and the sounds of her boot heels stomping across the floorboards died down. Another girl named Hailey Singh joined her, the pair of them sitting on either side of me on the couch. My head felt like a pendulum, my face swinging back and forth between the two girls as they each shared stories of the previous time Lydia had graced the halls of St. Agnes.

"I saw her rip a chunk of hair from this girl's head once," Hailey whispered. "Left her lying on the floor bleeding, right over there." She pointed to a spot near the television. "You can still see the blood stain if you look really close."

"What about Samantha?" Sarah asked. "Remember her?"

"Oh, yes," Hailey said with an added bit of dramatic fear. "Pushed the poor girl right down the stairs."

"What?" I couldn't believe what I was hearing, and at one point, I wondered whether they were simply pulling my leg for a bit of fun. "Did she get in trouble?"

"Not always," Sarah whispered. "Most of the time, the girls are too scared to tell the truth, like Samantha. She told Sister Alice that she *tripped* and fell down the stairs."

"She's going to kill me, isn't she?" I asked, staring at the space between the television screen and me.

"Probably," Hailey said and headed over to where a group was starting a new game of Monopoly.

"What am I going to do?" I asked Sarah once we were mostly alone.

Despair doesn't even begin to describe how I felt, especially after the way I had been practically worshipped for the previous couple of days. It was as if my world had suddenly transitioned from night to day in an instant, the dark shadow of a bully blocking out everything else in my life. Within minutes of her stepping into my life, I could think of nothing else, and hearing about her previous victims didn't help.

"You could always go and talk to Sister Alice," Sarah suggested, and while she might have been right, I knew deep inside that this was one situation I had to sort out for myself.

"How has that worked out for the others?" I asked, and Sarah didn't answer with words but instead, by casting her eyes down. "Yeah, that's what I thought," I said.

"Well, you'll be OK as long as you're not alone."

"How am I going to achieve that?" I asked. "It's not like I can have you and the others with me all the time."

"Just hang out in here as much as you can," Sarah said, and before I could answer, the girl of the moment came back.

Lydia walked into the room wearing the biggest smirk. A couple of girls followed her, and it took me a minute to recognize them as the ones who had been sitting on one of the top bunks when Sister Celia had taken me to the bedroom when I first arrived. Sarah groaned when she saw the three of them walk in and sit on one of the couches at the far end of the room.

For the first few minutes, the three of them just sat there talking, but hiding their mouths behind their hands and occasionally looking over at us. The smirking remained, of course, and I could sense that their attempts to intimidate me wouldn't simply go away. They were settling in for the long game, probably initiated by Lydia, who seemed hell bent on bullying me.

"You're not scaring us," Sarah called out defiantly, and Lydia immediately began to laugh, the other two following close behind.

"We're not *trying* to," one of the other girls called back, her tone contemptuous as she slowly enunciated each word.

That's when something curious happened. The room seemed to divide itself into two sides, each taking an interest in the other. Several of the girls playing Monopoly called for Lydia to join them, and when she suggested they play cards instead, four of the five girls abandoned the board game and joined the new group. Hailey and another girl briefly sat alone before walking back to where we were sitting.

"Lost your players, huh?" Sarah asked while watching the other group sit in a circle and start dealing cards.

"She's a bitch," Hailey whispered under her breath, several of the younger girls staring at her with their mouths dropped in shock at hearing the word. Hailey looked at them and shrugged. "Well, she is."

"Yes, she is," Sarah said in total agreement, although I noticed how neither of them wanted anybody else to hear, especially those seated on the opposite side of the room.

For me, I think that moment right there, sitting in that rec room surrounded by friends, was the last time I can remember my life being normal. And by normal, I mean a life where I wasn't constantly living in fear, either from bullies, or starving to death, or fearing for my life in general. That moment, sitting in that room as a naive seven year old girl, was the last time I remember ever feeling that deceptive shield of what we call childhood. That was the day my innocence faded away, exposing me to the harsh realities of life inside a system that didn't care whether I lived or died.

CHAPTER 5

Lydia Nutworth made it her duty to ensure I lived in the most miserable state of consciousness imaginable. She took great pleasure in not only recruiting those willing to help her, but she also meticulously planned ways for me to fall into their traps, which she then relished in watching play out in vivid detail. You might think that the bullying took time to really get going, but the truth is, her assault on my life began just seven hours after her arrival back at St. Agnes.

The first attack, if you could call it that, proved to be minor, occurring during dinner when she flicked a glob of mushy peas in my direction, which subsequently splattered across my forehead with a loud thwack. Her table exploded into laughter, and I saw the look of utter delight on Lydia's face as she cackled with glee. Sister Hope, the supervisor for the evening, had been busy talking with Deloris, and when she heard the uproar and turned around, she found the entire room erupting with laughter.

The second attack took things to a whole new level when, shortly before lights out, someone threw a plastic water bottle across the room that skidded over one bunk bed, hit the post of another, and ricocheted into the side of my head. I swear I saw stars suddenly explode before my eyes as pain shot through my ear. The laughter I heard came from somewhere on the other side of the room, although I couldn't see who. Sarah's face appeared next to me when she looked over the edge of the bed.

"Are you OK?" she asked, and while the throbbing did feel like fingers painfully grabbing the inside of my brain, I didn't want to openly admit that it hurt.

"I'm fine," I said and rolled over, figuring it was safer to face the wall than risk getting a second object thrown at me. A few minutes later, Sister Hope walked through the room during her final rounds and eventually turned the light off.

I lay in the darkness listening to more snickers coming from somewhere on the other side of the room, although I was beginning to recognize the voices behind the laughter. Thankfully, Lydia wasn't assigned to our room, but two of her closest allies were. Polly Wells and Jane Rowe would prove to be almost as challenging as Lydia, perhaps even marginally worse, considering they practically lived right next to me. There was no escaping for me, it seemed, not from girls intent on making my life a living hell.

The first Monday after my arrival, Sister Celia summoned me to her office first thing in the morning and spent the first few minutes having me try on one piece of school uniform after another in an attempt to get me fitted with a complete set. The hand-me-downs weren't exactly new, with some of the clothing looking ready for permanent retirement, but I didn't mind. I'd never owned a uniform before, and having one meant I didn't need to worry about which clothes to wear to school, the way I did back in my previous school.

Once breakfast was over, Sister Hope personally escorted me to school, with the rest of the girls following close behind for the three-block journey. Each time we crossed the street, the nun held me back while the rest of the group walked to the other side before her, and I followed. Lydia, Polly, and Jane made sure to snicker when they walked past, and I think I heard one of them whisper,

"Baby needs her hand held," when they walked past. I felt my cheeks burn with embarrassment, but it was short-lived.

While the rest of the kids scattered the second they entered the school yard, I got escorted to the main reception area, where Sister Hope finalized my enrollment with a few signatures. The woman working the counter brought a pile of books out from a storeroom and stuffed them into a bag, which she ultimately handed to me.

"Welcome to Brimvale," she said with a warm smile, probably one of the few genuine smiles I'd seen in almost a week.

"Thank you," I said as I took the bag and slung it over my shoulder, hoping my own smile didn't appear too forced.

"Your first lesson will be with Mr. Thurston's Maths class," the lady said and pointed to a nearby hallway. "It's the fourth door on the left. You may as well head there now, as the bell will ring shortly anyway." Again, she smiled, which I returned.

"I'll see you this afternoon," Sister Hope said with a stern tone, and when I gave her a smile, I saw her lips physically tighten.

A part of me wondered whether the nuns' facial expressions were more pronounced because their faces were the only parts visible and the only parts I could focus on. It just felt like all of them, except Sister Alice, had any positive emotions towards us, almost as if we really were just an inconvenient nuisance to them. Either that, or it was personal, and all of that negativity was aimed at me specifically.

"Don't be silly," Sarah told me later that day when I put the idea to her. "They're like that with everybody." I wasn't so sure.

Mr. Thurston turned out to be more of the same, a similar frown of unbridled frustration on his face the entire duration of the hour-long class. He did make me stand up and introduce myself to the entire room at the very beginning, but thankfully, none of the kids but Sarah were in my class. I would have practically died if either Lydia or her two friends had been there. Thankfully, maths had always been something of a strong suit for me. I just knew numbers and normally proved myself to be at a skillset several levels above the rest of my classmates, which Mr. Thurston discovered within the first twenty minutes.

English with Mrs. Lewiston was the second class for the day, and while I did have Jenny Rowe in the room, the teacher kicked her out within the first five minutes for throwing a scrunched-up ball of soaked paper at me. I knew she would find a way of blaming me for her getting removed from the class, but I didn't care, not when I got to spend an hour listening to the teacher reading a book to the class. The story had already been going for a couple of lessons, which meant I had no clue what it was about, but it felt good just to close my eyes and listen.

I met Sarah and a couple of her friends out in the playground during the lunch break, and as we sat in a circle on the grass eating our sandwiches, she pointed out several people for me to watch out for. As it turned out, the school had several bullies, and all just as venomous as Lydia, if not worse.

"Oh, and don't forget about Katherine," one of Sarah's friends said when a rather large girl emerged from one of the nearby doorways. They all looked over, and Sarah nodded.

"Yeah, you're right," she said before looking at me. "See that girl over there? She likes to steal people's food, and she also likes to pretend to be your friend and then hit you for no reason."

A torrential downpour ended up cutting our outside time short, and we headed back to the classrooms ten minutes before the official end of lunch. I stopped by the bathrooms along the way and told Sarah I'd meet up with her after school, since we didn't share either of our afternoon classes, and she gave me a one-armed hug before continuing on.

It was while washing my hands after finishing my business that I realized the error of my ways when I heard a giggle from the doorway. I looked over and immediately felt the beating in my chest pick up, with three faces staring back at me. I tried to ignore them by finishing washing my hands, but there was no escape, not when I had effectively walked into a dead end.

"Well, look who it is," Lydia snickered as she handed her schoolbag to one of the others. "The bed stealer."

"I didn't steal your bed," I said as I turned off the tap and looked at her. "Sister Celia told me that is where I had to sleep."

"You should have asked for another," Lydia said, the familiar smirk returning.

"As if I knew who had slept there before," I said, trying to sound completely disinterested in the conversation, but the truth is, I was scared.

"Not my problem," Lydia said and stopped just a couple of feet from me, her fists clenched up into tight balls.

"What are you going to do? Hit me?" I returned the smirk. "So, it's not about the bed, but more about you needing to be tough in front of your friends," I said, hoping to embarrass her into submission. "Must be really brave to gang up on someone three to one."

"Who's ganging up?" Lydia sked, looking behind her. "It looks like it's just you and me here." More snickering from behind her.

"I'm not going to fight you," I said, feeling my own fists balling up and trying to relax them. I didn't want to antagonize the situation.

"Suit yourself," Lydia said and lunged forward.

"What is going on in here?" an authoritative voice suddenly called out just as a fist swung for my face. I managed to pull back just in time before Lydia reeled her hand back in and spun around to face Mrs. Lewiston, who stood at the door. Lydia froze for a second before she managed to free herself from the initial shock.

"I was just welcoming the new girl," Lydia said as she walked back to where her two friends stood.

"Wait for me outside," Lewiston demanded, the woman's transformation from friendly teacher to stone-faced controller instant. I didn't see Lydia's face on account of the fact that she was walking away from me, but her "Yes, Ma'am" sounded just as I imagined her expression to have been.

Lewiston watched the three girls leave and turn back to me until the door had closed again. Only then did she take a couple of steps towards me.

"I'm going to give you the benefit of the doubt that you didn't do anything to antagonize them," she said. "And in the future, you'd be wiser to use the student bathroom next to the staffroom. There's less chance of…issues going to happen."

"Yes, Ma'am," I said, considered adding a thank you, and quickly decided it was best just to let the matter rest.

That first day of school had been eye-opening on so many levels, and not just because it had been my first and everything felt so new to me. It was because of the realization that I had literally nowhere to run from the bullies now living in my life. Home, school, playtime, it was all the same, and my existence now revolved around trying my best to avoid getting my butt handed to me.

The walk back to St. Agnes that afternoon felt like a stark contrast to the morning. Now that I had an awareness of what each subsequent day would look like, I lacked the same sense of excitement I had carried with me earlier in the day. The real problem I had, and you have to remember that I looked at the issue with a seven-year-old's mind, was that I had nobody else to help me. The world I had once known and lived in had effectively come to an end.

CHAPTER 6

I could go through and describe each and every day of my existence for you, but I doubt you'd find what I have to share very interesting, at least not for the majority of the days. The problem is that as a kid, my world was far more influenced by those to whom I didn't matter than those who I did. Most kids grow up in a home where at least a mother, or father, or both, or both with siblings, or an aunt or uncle, will raise them. Maybe a grandma or two, plus any number of iterations. Not so for me.

St. Agnes wasn't a home where anybody truly loved me the way family did. I had a couple of friends, sure, but everyone else didn't care whether I was there or not. Their lives would have continued on regardless, without so much as a blink. I doubt even Sarah would have spent too much time fretting over me leaving before completely forgetting about me. You could say that life in the system is similar to living in your own individual bubble, and only a select few will ever visit you inside that bubble. For the most part, they simply stick your bubble on top of other ones and keep you stacked in a kind of bookshelf as a group to make it easier to keep an eye on you.

Some days, it honestly felt like I was nothing more than a

number to those around me, the ninth name called out from the attendance sheet each morning, or the fifteenth in line at dinner. I might be the third when playing four-square, or the *second* when someone needed a partner in whatever game was being played, like, "Hey, Emma, want to be Beth's second for Pictionary?" You get the idea.

I think those first couple of months proved to be the hardest for me, in terms of getting my head around the kind of world I was now a part of. Sure, I faced struggles in the subsequent years as well, but those were of a completely different nature and endured by someone already wearing the scars that come with living within the system. Those first months, however? Those were the days when I felt my body being slowly dipped into a tub full of acid designed to eat away at the very heart of my being…my soul.

I once heard a story about a friend of mine who signed up for the Navy. Bruce Ackerman, his name is. I met him at a bar in Paris, not that that has any bearing on what I'm about to tell you. He was telling me about how his commanding officer once ordered him and another sailor to clean a communal bathroom with nothing but a toothbrush and soap. I laughed at him, thinking he was kidding.

"No, it's not a joke," he said as he held a hand up defensively. "There's a reason why they make you do shit like that."

"What possible reason could there be?" I asked him, and what he told me at the time, reminded me of those first few months I spent at St. Agnes.

"It has nothing to do with the actual task," he said. "They get you to do all sorts of weird things, like paint rocks white, maybe get you to dig a random hole and then fill it up again, stuff like that."

"Why?"

"Because they want you to be the kind of person who follows orders without question," was what he said. "They slowly strip away your questions so that you will follow orders. In the heat of battle, there's no time for questions. Questions can get people killed."

That is exactly how I looked back at those first few months at that home, with my personality slowly stripped of whatever individuality I had. The love from a family, the independence that comes with living alone in a bedroom, the attention one gets when an only child or one of two or three. Kids living with families live vastly different lives from those living in a place like St. Agnes. That type of existence feels more like survival, where you are forced to fight for every bit of life, from the food you need to the little snippets of joy brought through watching television or playing a video game. You weren't guaranteed a seat unless you fought for it, sometimes physically, when people like Lydia Nutworth wanted to take it from you.

It became almost unbearable for me during those first couple of months, when I would cry myself to sleep almost every night. It became so common that I would hide a roll of toilet tissue under my pillow, just so I had enough to help with the clean up. I didn't sob outwardly, of course, the tears falling silently for more than an hour at times. I had already been nicknamed Cry Baby on account of bursting into tears when Lydia managed to slam a door on my fingers, the impact causing three of my nails to turn black and eventually fall off. Who wouldn't have cried at such a painful event, and yet, thanks to Lydia's relentless teasing about my crying, the rest of her followers quickly adopted the moniker for me.

When Sister Alice heard two of the girls call me Cry Baby, she pulled them aside and gave them a stern talking to, and while I was hopeful they might ease up on the teasing, they simply flipped the script and called me CB for short. The name quickly spread, and it wasn't long before it felt like everybody was using it.

The fingers caught in the door weren't the only physical injuries I suffered during those first few months. Someone tripped me in the shower, and I fell to the floor hard. Another time, a person knocked a plate of food out of my hand, and everyone laughed and pointed at me in the dining room. And then...and then there was the day something actually broke my nose.

That Friday began like any other at school, with Mrs. Lewiston taking roll call and marking all the names off before transitioning the class to creating simple limericks. She had been focusing on poetry all week, and we had been given free time to create our own the previous day. That Friday, she had us read them out in front of the class, and while extremely nervous, I had a good feeling because Mrs. Lewiston had already commented about how much she loved what I had written.

With the order of reading determined by where we sat, and the starting point at the back of the room, I ended up last, since I sat on the left side of the front row. That hour felt like one of the longest of my life as I felt my insides knot tighter and tighter each time another student went up, read their work, and sat back down. I could see similar nerves on each of their faces, but none of them compared to my own.

When the moment finally arrived, I felt every pair of eyes watching me as I stood and walked to the front of the class, the book held against my chest like a shield. I felt the heat in my cheeks rising to the very tips of my ears as I could barely look up from the page once I began reading. The silence felt overwhelming, the beating in my chest hard enough for me to feel it in my temples.

"Go ahead, Emma," Mrs. Lewiston said when I took a little too long to start. You'd think I would try to rush through it so I could sit back down, but I swear it felt like my mouth had frozen shut, refusing to open to let any of the words come out. Someone snickered at the back of the room, and the heat in my cheeks intensified.

"T-t-the sun shone down on the flower bed," I began, the words coming out all shaky. "Lighting up colours like blue and red. The wind made them sway, the bees flew away, and helped the flowers' seeds to spread."

A couple of kids laughed, but Mrs. Lewiston immediately called for them to be quiet before turning to me.

"That was very well done," she said. "I could picture the actual flowers swaying in the wind, and that's what poetry is all about." She turned to the class. "When you can picture someone's words, that's when you know you've heard something special." And then back to me, "Very well done."

I heard a few quiet remarks from the back row when I retook my seat, but I ignored them, more focused on getting the colour in my cheeks to subside. The bell went off a few minutes later, and I joined the rush of people leaving the classroom, thankful to leave the nerves and moment of embarrassment behind. Little did I know that I was actually walking to something far worse.

Our school consisted of two main buildings joined by a central walkway that stretched from the street fronting our school to the playing fields at the back. My plan had been to walk out onto the playground, find Sarah, and sit with her while eating our lunch, just as I had done almost every day since starting at the school. I walked along the central corridor surrounded by streams of other people, with my mind still focused on the public reading. Call it relief, the adrenaline still charging through my system, but slowly settling down again. Mrs. Lewiston's comment had actually given me quite a confidence boost, so much so that I was smiling as I walked.

I never saw what hit me until the pain exploded in the middle of my face without warning. One second, I had reached the end of the corridor and was scanning the different groups of kids out on the grass, the next, brilliant white heat temporarily blinded me as a wave of agony rippled outward. The scream felt like it had been pushed out of me as my knees immediately buckled. I reached out to steady myself, feeling for the walls. Tears of pain filled my eyes, and ran down my face as the shock kept any hint of crying away.

"Are you OK?" an unknown voice asked me, and I remember shaking my head as something warm ran across my lips.

Wiping a hand across my face, I saw the streak of blood mixed with the increasing tears, and when I tried to wipe more away, I looked out to the field where a group of girls stood in a huddle with a familiar face in the very middle. To my shock, some of them were openly laughing, a couple pointing me out to those who hadn't spotted me. It took another wipe for me to clear up my vision, and that's when I looked down and saw the yo-yo someone had thrown.

The force of the impact broke my nose, and I had to make a trip to the hospital with one of the teachers. We sat in the emergency room for close to four hours before I managed to see a doctor, and when I finally ended up back at St. Agnes shortly after lights out, the whispers reached out to me from the shadows. Girls teased me the second Sister Alice left, mocking me from the shadows as if I hadn't had enough already.

There's only so much noise a pillow will block out when held over one's head, and that night, I tried my hardest to block out the most. I think that was also the first night I realized my nightly sobs weren't as private as I first believed, as I heard comments along the lines of, *There she goes again*. It felt like no matter how hard I tried to be nice, to be friendly and open, the world just turned away from me a little bit more, maybe hoping I would just disappear.

CHAPTER 7

Eight weeks after arriving at St. Agnes, a girl named Heather Porter moved into one of the upstairs bedrooms and immediately turned the place on its head. It was obvious from the very beginning that she wasn't like the other kids. Unlike everyone else who always appeared defeated and angry, she had spirit, a kind of energy many gravitated towards, and not because they were scared of her, like Lydia Nutworth. No, Heather made friends because people genuinely liked her and wanted to be with her.

The other thing I should probably tell you about Heather is that she also had confidence, the kind that intimidated those who used fear to push others around. Lydia, Polly, Jane, Erica Muntz…all the girls who craved attention and used fear to intimidate smaller and younger kids now had a real opponent, someone who didn't take bullshit. Heather not only stood up to them when they first tried to get in her face, but she also actively hunted them, calling out to them the way they used to do to me.

The first afternoon she spent in the rec room with us, Heather came and sat next to me on the couch as I watched a movie on the TV alone. It was rare to find the TV off and nobody already claiming the space, so I used the opportunity to watch one of the few movies I actually enjoyed, Sailor Moon. The cover of the tape was completely worn out and the label torn off, but someone had used a pencil to write the title on the small strip of paper still clinging to the front of the tape. I fell in love the first time I watched it, the show transporting me away from the misery of my life.

"Sailor Moon, huh?" Heather said as she sat cross-legged on the opposite side of the couch.

I looked over at her but didn't say anything, still too shy and unsure about her. I had seen her easily put Lydia in her place an hour or so earlier, and I still hadn't made up my mind as to whether she would be more trouble for me. It felt as if the bullies had been lining up to get their claws into me, and I didn't want to openly invite another one in.

"Have you seen the movie?" Heather asked, and I shook my head.

"This tape is all they have here," I said, showing her the cover and pointing to the three episodes printed on the back.

"Damn shame," she said. "The movie is fantastic. The show is so much better, too. I wish you could see the entire series." She looked over at me. "Who is your favourite?"

"Sailor Moon," I said. "But I do like Sailor Mars as well."

"Sailor Mars is cool. I'm more of a Sailor Jupiter myself, although you can't go past Moon." That was when she reached over and held her hand out like a real grown-up. "I'm Heather."

"Emma," I said as we shook. Her skin felt unusually cold, and she must have seen my reaction.

"I get cold hands all the time," she said. "Even in the middle of summer. Some people say it's due to poor circulation, but my mum used to tell me that cold hands mean a warm heart."

She smiled warmly, and it was perhaps the very first time since arriving at the hime myself that I genuinely felt someone liked me.

"I get cold hands too," I said, although it might have been a bit of an exaggeration. I think she knew, but didn't say anything bad, the way some of the other girls might have.

"Then you must have a warm heart as well," was what she said.

Heather told me that she had just turned fourteen and had spent most of her life in the system, although she used to live in Carlisle, a city in the very north of the country. Her previous foster mum moved to London a year earlier for work, but when a promotion gave her the opportunity to move to New York, an unwanted foster child didn't factor into her plans.

"She told me that I would just be extra baggage she didn't need," Heather told me while continuing to share her story with me after dinner. "I sometimes wonder what it would have been like to travel to a different country."

"That's what I'm going to do one day," I told her as we lay on our bellies on the floor in front of the television. "I'm going to travel the world."

"I believe you will," Heather said.

I think we must have spent most afternoons during the week together, and most days on the weekends, as well. We became friends, much closer than I had ever felt with Sarah. She brought with her a new kind of positivity I hadn't experienced before, not even when living in the home of a family I believed to have loved me. That's the problem with not having anything to compare it to, because once Heather entered my life, she became the person I compared everyone else to.

You are probably picturing a sweet and innocent girl, maybe with braces, a neat ponytail, and always well presented. The problem is that's not Heather. She wasn't sweet and innocent at all. I sometimes watched her go looking for trouble, especially when something had put her in a bad mood. She would actually go and see out Lydia or Polly, or one of the other girls, just to pick a fight, and not just a verbal one. Heather liked to get hands-on, not just with girls. She once told me that a boy at her school tried to steal her lunch, and she ended up beating him up hard enough for him to need a trip to the hospital.

"He deserved it," she said while popping jelly babies into her mouth one at a time as we sat on the couch. "That's how you beat them, Em. Never show them weakness."

As for the ponytail, Heather didn't have one. She actually didn't have any hair to speak of, aside from a very short stubble.

"Don't have to worry about what it looks like when it's this short," she used to say. "And I don't need to worry about shampoo, or conditioner, or haircuts at all." She'd tap the side of her head with a finger and grin at me. "That's what I call using your brain."

She spoke truth, and shared it in a way that made her so much more likeable. I felt like Heather was the sister I should have been born with, a family member with whom I could have lived and shared so much. Yes, she might have lived in a room on another floor, but we still hung out as if we shared the same bedroom. We ate our meals together, walked to school together, and she even snuck down into my room after dark and lay in bed with me.

The days turned into weeks and weeks into months, with life finally passing me by with a kind of uniform structure. The bullying that had plagued me for weeks before Heather's arrival faded away completely. Lydia eventually left St. Agnes, which wasn't a great loss to most, although Polly and Jane felt the immediate repercussions of her departure. Many of the girls they had picked on immediately turned on them, and they ended up as the eventual outcasts. I didn't care. To me, the universe had decided to return the kind of torment they had dished out onto so many others, and I doubt many of us felt sorry for them.

There was this one time, though, where Heather surprised me with a night I can never forget. It happened completely out of the blue, and I have to admit that it felt as if all the magic of childhood had come at once. Do you remember how I shared that Heather would sometimes come to my room after lights-out and lie beside me as we whispered about anything and everything? Well, it became so common that even the night supervisors gave up trying to stop her, including Sister Alice. They said that as long as we didn't annoy anybody and kept our voices down, then she would be okay with it.

On this particular night, Heather didn't even bother going to her bedroom first, the way she usually did. When Sister Rose came through just before nine on her final rounds, she gave Heather and me a kind of sigh, frowned, and just continued on.

"Thank you, Ma'am," Heather whispered to her just before she walked out of earshot, and the nun waved the apology away.

I moved closer to the wall, raised the blanket and waited for Heather to climb in beside me before lowering the covers again. Around us, others continued getting ready for bed until the lights eventually snapped off. A couple of people sighed when the shadows interrupted final conversations or the final few words of whatever book they were reading, but they didn't last long. A heavy silence descended over the room within minutes, and not long after, soft snores began to rise and fall somewhere out in the darkness.

The conversation between Heather and me also faded out almost immediately, and I could feel my friend lying motionless beside me. I could just make out the silhouette of her face as she lay on her back, staring up at the ceiling. I caught the occasional blinking, which seemed pretty normal. After wishing her a good night, I closed my eyes.

What nobody ever came right out and said was why Heather came and lay in my bed with me. The thing is, she didn't stay there all night. She'd usually start off lying next to me, but then at some point after I fell asleep, she would sneak back up to her own bed on the third floor. I don't know if anybody ever saw her, but by the time I woke up, she was usually gone. Not so, this particular night.

I did nod off relatively quickly as it had been quite a long day. Saturdays usually were, especially when we found something positive to do within the group, like a team-style game, or some form of sports we played out in the yard. That night, I went to bed expecting to fall asleep almost immediately and wake up late the next morning to sunshine streaming in through the worn-out curtain beside my bed. That's not what happened.

"Em, wake up, geez," were the first words I heard when I felt myself being shaken repeatedly. My eyes felt impossibly heavy, and I could have sworn the fine line between dream and reality had been breached, with neither feeling real. "Em, come on, now," the voice repeated with a whisperish hiss. I managed to open one of my eyes and make out the familiar silhouette, but Heather's voice still didn't sound real. That was when she pinched my inside leg.

"Ouch," I cried out, and an invisible hand slapped across my mouth, blocking the sound and deflecting it back down my throat like an echo.

"Shhh," Heather whispered. "You'll wake the others."

"What's going on?" I asked, and she leaned in close enough for me to feel her breath on my ear.

"Want to come with me on a little adventure?"

Something buzzed inside me, a kind of adrenaline-fueled excitement waking up as I saw Heather hold a finger to her mouth and shush me. I nodded and watched as she carefully lifted the blanket back and slowly swung her legs over the edge before she inched her way off the bunk. Her head briefly paused in midair as she found her footing on the lower bunk, and then disappeared altogether. I rolled closer to the edge and peered over to see her drop all the way to the floor and reach underneath the lower bed. When I saw her pull some kind of bag out, I realised this wasn't some spur-of-the-moment decision.

"Come on," Heather hissed, the words barely audible as she mouthed them more than she spoke them, although I couldn't see her lips. I think I heard the sound reverberating somewhere deep inside her chest rather than actually rising into the air.

I twisted myself around the same way Heather had and slid off the top bunk, using the lower bed to step down. I felt Heather's hand on my back as she helped to steady me, and once I had my feet firmly on the floor, she again reminded me to be quiet with a finger held to her mouth.

With the bag slung over her shoulder, and one hand holding my arm, Heather slowly crept between the bunks towards the door. It wasn't uncommon for girls to wake up in the middle of the night to take bathroom trips, and so her opening the door didn't really sound out of the ordinary. It did creak somewhat, but she knew how far to open it before pushing me through the gap and into the darkened hallway beyond.

I expected her to push me towards the main staircase, but instead, Heather pulled me the other way, heading down the far end of the hallway where a single window stood at the very end. I could have sworn the window had been nailed permanently shut, but she managed to open it with ease. After peering out to make sure the coast was clear, Heather raised a leg and began to climb out onto a small landing I never knew existed. Once we both stood outside, and the window was again closed, Heather pointed to a trestle that had been fixed to the wall, with a vine-type plant growing every which way.

"Wait," she suddenly said and pulled me back against the wall. A shadow appeared below, the shape slowly walking along the tiny path that wound through that part of the yard. Hailey hung on tightly to my arm as Max, the security guy, walked his usual patrol. If he had spotted us, our night would have come to a very premature end.

Hailey waited a few minutes after Max disappeared before she pointed to the trestle and pulled me a little forward.

"OK, go now, but be careful," she whispered.

It took a bit of manoeuvring, but we both managed to work our way down, my friend making it look way too easy, and while I never came right out and asked her, I wondered just how many times she had used the escape route. This was not the night I imagined for myself, and as we stood in the moonlight next to the garden bed, I wondered how much crazier it would get.

"Here, take these," Heather said when she opened the bag and reached into it. She pulled a bundle of something, and while it was too dark to see what it was, I could feel the soft fabric of a jumper. "Go behind that bush over there and get changed, but do it quickly."

I didn't answer her, but I did smile with excitement. This wasn't something I had ever done, and the idea that Heather might have planned something bad never crossed my mind. Once I had thrown on the jeans, jumper, and shoes, I went back to the same spot where Heather was putting on a jacket.

"Where are we going?" I asked, sure to keep my voice low. She didn't answer me, or at least not until we had reached the street and walked about half a block down the road.

The street lights were spaced about thirty or so metres apart and not overly powerful, which meant we could walk most of the way while hidden by shadows. Hailey held my hand, with the other holding one of the straps of the bag she had slung over her shoulder again.

"A surprise," she finally said when we reached the second cross street and turned left.

Never in my wildest dreams would I have guessed where she took me. Not only had I never been inside a real movie theatre before, but who would have thought that the first movie I would ever see would be something I had dreamed about for so long.

"Here we are," Heather eventually said when we reached another corner and cut across the street towards a large building. She steered us towards an alley, checked her watch and then pulled me into a small thicket of bushes. "Just have to wait a second," she whispered.

I felt scared, sitting there hidden in the dark like that, but a small part of me couldn't ignore the excitement either. We watched the side of the building where a single door stood closed, and I felt Heather tense as it eventually opened.

"Shhh," she said softly as a man dressed in a uniform walked out, propping a nearby brick between the door and the frame before lighting a cigarette. I could see the red embers light up his face as he puffed a few times. "One second," Heather whispered, and held my arm tight while watching the man slowly walk down the alley. "OK, now," she said and pulled me along as she pushed herself out of the bushes.

We rushed across the narrow alley and half-ran into the doorway. A dark corridor greeted us, and Heather kept a tight grip on me as she navigated our way through a door and down a second corridor. I could hear sounds of explosions and gunfire coming from various directions before a song faded in from a different one of the cinemas, and loud voices from another. But nothing, absolutely nothing, could compete with that incredible smell of fresh popcorn hanging in the air.

When we reached a staircase, Heather first paused and looked up, holding me back while she made sure the coast was clear. Only when she was sure did she release her hold and push me up.

"OK, go, go, go," she muttered, looking back over her shoulder while running up the staircase.

We reached another hallway, only this time, she stopped in front of the very first door, took a deep breath and tried the handle. It looked to turn easily, but rather than pull the door open to allow us entry, Heather only pulled it out a few inches before peering inside. I could hear voices, but not the sort amplified by modern technology.

"Stay close," Heather murmured and pushed inside.

At first, I couldn't see a thing; the material I could feel brushing against my face was too thick to allow any light through. We slowly crept along a wall, Heather pulling me along beside her until she found a gap in the curtain and carefully pulled the two ends apart. She pulled me slightly ahead of herself and leaned in close.

"Sit there," she whispered, and I suddenly found myself standing between a couple of rows of seats near the back of a movie theatre.

The seats Heather had taken us to were located up on a small landing above the main area, and I could see dozens of people seated below us. The screen showed a static image of an old-style movie reel with the words It's Showtime in gold lettering underneath. Heather sat down beside me as we took our seats in the very back row of that second-floor gallery, a level that had been cordoned off for renovations.

Once we were seated, Heather opened her bag again and pulled out a couple of bottles of Cola, a bag of crisps, and two bags of chocolate M&Ms.

"Gotta have snacks, right?" She asked with bemusement, handed me a drink and popped the top off her own.

"This isn't your first time here, is it?" I asked, nervously taking the drink. She shook her head and quietly laughed.

"Sometimes, you have to take action if you want to live like the rest of the world," she said, and threw a handful of M&Ms into her mouth.

While I can't tell you what previews came on before the main movie on account of my memory losing their names, I can tell you the feeling of absolute astonishment I felt when the opening credits to Sailor Moon S began to roll. I looked from the screen to Heather and back again with complete surprise, and the smile she flashed back at me is one I can never forget. She seemed so pleased with herself, and while I know that she would have seen the happiness on my face, I don't think she ever quite knew just how much that one night with her truly meant to me.

CHAPTER 8

Heather Porter probably played more of a role in shaping my childhood than any other person I can remember. She did things in a very different way, lived her life with so much more adventurous flair than the rest of the girls at St. Agnes. She truly was the sister I never had, and I can only imagine how different my life would have been if we had remained as close as we were that night at the cinema.

If you expect me to tell you that the night ended up being some perfect adventure that brought our friendship even closer together, then I'm sorry to burst your bubble. Real life rarely follows the rags-to-riches storyline as seen in so many Hollywood movies, and while that night with Heather might have been one of the best nights of my life up until that point, it ended up also being the worst.

I'm not sure if someone saw us sitting up in the second-floor gallery and reported us, or whether the security guy just happened to catch us in the hallway by accident, but it felt like he was waiting for us when we walked out of the door after the movie. He escorted us to a ground-floor office where he made us sit on a couple of seats, demanded to know our address and parents' names, and then proceeded to phone the police when we refused to answer any of his questions. I would have probably answered them all were it not for Heather telling me to be quiet.

When the police turned up, they separated Heather and me, and it took about a minute for me to break down when the lady police officer questioned me. I don't think Heather ever blamed me for doing so. She held me close during the subsequent car ride back to St. Agnes, with one arm around my shoulders and a hand holding mine. She whispered little reassurances into my ear, telling me everything would be OK. At one point, she even apologised for putting me through the ordeal, and I immediately told her she hadn't done a thing wrong. Her even thinking that she had saddened me.

That night had been one of the most adventurous nights of my life, and I must have replayed each and every moment a thousand times over in the subsequent years. Everything from the way I felt when she first shook me awake, to standing on that ledge watching the security guard walking by, to the smell of the popcorn in the air of the movie theatre. I can still hear the sounds of the explosions from some action movie, and the voices arguing from one of the other theatres. I can still feel my friend guiding me along every inch of the hallway, the road, the footpath, and the alleyway.

It hadn't just been an adventure to me. It felt like an awakening, my soul experiencing for the first time what it meant to be free. No grown-ups constantly telling me how to act, how to behave, what I could and couldn't do. I had tasted a small sample of the world outside of my own existence, where people enjoyed escaping into other worlds with the magic of movies, and where any future could be dreamed of without judgment. If only I could have hung onto that feeling of freedom for a bit longer, but like I said before, happy endings rarely happen in the real world, and the real world was where my life remained.

"Go to your beds," Sister Celia demanded once the two officers left us alone with the nun in the foyer of the building. "We shall discuss this further in the morning."

It must have been way past midnight by that point. I could somehow feel the late hour in the air, the look of sleep on both Sister Celia and Sister Alice's faces evident. I couldn't picture the shock on their faces when they heard of our little escapade, but there was definitely some hint of familiarity that told me this hadn't been the first time they faced such a scenario. If I had known then what I know now, perhaps I would have refused to go with Heather, maybe told her that it would be best to remain in bed and just fall asleep like everybody else. Maybe then, we could have avoided all the heartache and confusion that filled our world the following day.

When I woke up that next morning, I first thought the previous night's events had been nothing more than a dream, the events just short of that real vividness. Sadly, it didn't take long for me to realise that it was the brain fog hanging over my brain that made the whole thing feel like a dream, and an audible groan shot out of me once I realised it had, in fact, been real. I closed my eyes again, hoping to escape back into some distracting dream, if only for another hour. Fate had other ideas.

What brought me back to reality were the voices I heard talking somewhere outside of my room. Sister Celia's usual authoritative drone was there, as well as a woman I immediately recognised, which is why I jumped out of bed. Panic gripped me as I recognised Claudette's much softer voice, although I did detect a hint of apprehension, which was what hurried me out to check on them.

The momentum with which I exited the room and onto the second-floor landing carried me all the way to the guard rail, my legs moving much too quickly for me to reverse. Sister Celia saw me and shook her head in disgust, but it was the other woman I was more interested in. A thought occurred to me, one that I didn't want to acknowledge but felt powerless to deflect. What if Claudette had come back for me?

"What have I told you about running in the house?" Sister Celia snapped as I rushed down the stairs. My feet tangled half a dozen steps from the bottom, and I completely ignored her as my hand shot out in panic to catch myself from falling the rest of the way.

"I promise I won't do it again," I cried, the tears welling up in my eyes as I couldn't think straight. I couldn't bear the thought of being taken away again, not so soon after meeting someone as special as Heather. It felt like I had waited my entire life for a friend like her, and now the universe wanted to take me away again. "Please, Sister, I swear I will be good. Just don't send me away."

"Don't be absurd, child," Sister Celia said with her usual tone of arrogance. "I have no intention of sending you anywhere but back to your room."

It wasn't her words that made me stop, nor the tone she used, but something made me freeze in front of her, a realisation that sent shivers through me. It was the look in her eyes I couldn't get away from. To me, it looked almost victorious, something about the glint of satisfaction flipping me off. I looked over my shoulder towards the front door and saw Claudette walking away.

"Let this be a lesson," Sister Celia said with that same arrogance in her tone, and that was when the truth hit me like a freight train, a truth I would have never expected were it not for the look on her face.

"No," I cried out, the understanding far too robust to ignore, and I ran for the door. I swear my feet barely touched the ground during that initial sprint. The nun did try to grab me, but I was too quick for her, gone like a rat in a cattery.

"You come back here, girl," Sister Celia called after me, but I wasn't about to stop, not when I had my friend to rescue.

I don't remember ever touching the door. I think I somehow willed it open before I got there, or I hit it so fast that it flung open so hard that it locked into place and remained standing wide open. I tried to see where my friend had gone, but the hedge blocked my view.

By the time I reached the bottom of the steps, Claudette had already climbed into her car, and despite my calling out, she never acknowledged my cries. I screamed as hard as my lungs allowed, the desperation harsh enough to burn my vocal chords. More tears rolled down my cheeks, some from the pain in my throat that felt like I'd swallowed a handful of sand, but more out of sheer anguish. I saw a shape move behind the backdoor window, and when it rolled down, Heather stared out at me with a smile.

"No," I cried out again. "Heather, no, come back."

The tears fell thick enough for the car to appear like it was moving through a wall of water, my legs desperately trying to get me to her. I screamed again and again, all the while waving for Heather to jump out, but she didn't. The security guard rushed me from behind, snatched one of my wrists into his powerful hands, and slid an arm under mine to lift me off the ground. I tried to fight him, but it was no good, my strength no match against his.

"Let's go," the guard said, dragging me along as I tried my hardest to resist. I knew it was futile, but that wasn't a reason enough to stop trying. I couldn't just stop trying, not after making one of the best friends of my life. I think the guard did feel sorry for me, because he didn't drag me back inside straight away. He hesitated, and at one point paused completely when I caught sight of my friend.

The last time I saw Heather, she kissed her hand and then waved it at me before calling out her final words, the final ones I ever heard her speak.

"Live it your way," was what she called back at me before the window went up and her arm disappeared. I remember still fighting to free myself when the car turned the next corner, and that was when I knew she had really gone. That was when I understood that my best friend wouldn't be coming back, not then and not ever.

I eventually did go back inside the house, but not before the guard brought me to the steps where Sister Celia stood waiting for me. Nothing could have made me look at her in that moment, and I think she enjoyed knowing how much anguish she had caused me. The guard set me down, but kept a hand firmly on my shoulder. I think he probably expected me to take off again, but my energy had effectively been used up, both physically and mentally. I had been beaten but not defeated.

"You will cease this obnoxious behaviour this very instant, young lady," Sister Celia said as she stared down at me. The guard stood silently behind me, his fingers digging into the soft part of my shoulder. "You will calm yourself down and return to your bed, where you will stay until the midday meal. If I hear so much as a peep out of you, I will send you down to Mr Taylor, and you can spend the rest of the day down in the basement. Do I make myself clear?"

Silence. My insides felt ready to explode, and I continued trying my hardest to keep the tears in check. If I had answered, I'm sure I would have lost control, which was why I held off. Thankfully, Sister Celia didn't expect me to answer. She simply nodded for the guard to let go of me, and once he did, I walked up the stairs, through the open doorway, and headed straight for the stairs. A couple of girls on kitchen duty stuck their heads out to see what was going on, but I ignored them as well, not even giving them the slightest look.

When I reached the bedroom, I could feel eyes watching me from other beds, but again, I ignored both the people and the whispers I could hear. I knew this wasn't the time for confrontations, not when I had already spent my energy on other battles. I think if I had gone in for the fight, I wouldn't have been able to stop myself, and that would have only made things worse.

Instead, I climbed up onto my bunk, pulled the covers over my head and faced the wall. I squeezed my eyes shut tight enough to keep out what little light did bleed through the fabric, and with my palms pressed tight against my ears, I blocked out the sounds as well. What I didn't know at the time, and wouldn't find out for several years, was that what I went through that day was grief, the same kind I would have felt if I had been old enough when my mother died. Losing my best friend like that felt like she had physically died, and with her never to return, in a way, I guess she really did.

CHAPTER 9

I don't think I ever fully recovered from losing Heather, not then and certainly not in the weeks and months that followed. When you think about losing someone close to you, I'm sure you will recall having the support of your family and friends, especially if you grew up in a home with parents who cared for you and understood the immense pain that goes along with the loss. Not so for me.

Growing up in the system for me meant no support from anybody, not even those who eventually called my friends. Nobody in those subsequent weeks and months came anywhere near to the bond I had shared with Heather. She felt like a sister, not that I knew what having an actual sister felt like, but I imagined it felt very close to what I experienced with Heather in my life.

In any case, the next few months rolled by with a kind of mundane blur. Not even Christmas festivities were enough to pull me from my depressed state, a state that kept me isolated and alone from almost every person at St. Agnes. The separation I felt wasn't just me keeping to myself. It felt as if I wasn't in the same world as those around me, a shadow caught in another dimension.

Everybody received a gift on the day, of course, given out by

Father Peter, who they said dressed up in the same worn-out costume year after year. He was the one who led the mass that morning, and after joining our home for lunch, we spent the first part of the afternoon huddled around the Christmas tree, awaiting our name to be called by the pretend Santa. Even Sister Celia managed a rare smile when Father Peter insisted she come up and receive a gift of her own. She didn't look too pleased with the scented candle pack she received, but that small bit of gratitude she showed did offer a glimpse into the person she could have been.

As for me, the gift I received could have been interpreted as a sign from the universe itself, fate sending a gift with a reminder that even my life deserved remembering. The diary I unwrapped wasn't exactly a top-shelf book with leather-bound covers and expensive gold-embroidered lettering. No, the diary I received that day looked more like something bought at Poundland, but I didn't care. The book had this pink vinyl-type covering, with the words Making Memories stencilled in black ink across the front cover's middle. It also had the silhouette of a girl sitting cross-legged underneath, with a book and pen in her hands, which sat on the strap one used to lock the book. A little keyhole sat where the girl's book was, and I found a golden key taped onto the plastic casing. The box also contained the pen, which made things easier, I guess, a cute pink and gold kind.

At first, I wasn't quite sure what to do with the diary. I had never owned one before, much less written down my day-to-day happenings. I mean, who in their right mind would want to read the goings-on about some unknown girl living in a foster home? Then it occurred to me that a diary may not have been solely for the purpose of writing down notes about each day. It could also serve as a kind of entity capable of listening to me the way a friend might, a non-judgmental friend who didn't try to offer answers or solutions. Wasn't that what a professional counsellor did?

At first, the notes I took had more to do with my feelings and moods, and how I reacted to various situations. I wrote down questions I had, not looking for answers but rather to keep them somewhere for later reference. After a few days of meaningless scribbling, I began to take things a little more seriously and started to share deeper emotions about certain situations, as well as write down little personal goals of mine. Before I knew it, the diary became my daily obsession, serving as my safe place that I kept with me all day long.

I still have that diary with me today, perhaps the only real possession I managed to hang onto in the subsequent years. I even used it to help me with writing these chapters for you, although its overall condition is a far cry from how it looked back on that cold and snowy winter's day. Back then, I kept the diary safe from the rigours of my day, but it eventually wore the scars of my journey, similar to those etched across my soul.

What I can tell you is that time is a curious thing when it comes to someone like me living in a place where relationships are sometimes measured by your worth to someone. People weighed up what benefit you brought into their lives, and if it didn't measure up, then you didn't matter to them. The time someone put into a relationship didn't matter so much as the time it took for them to benefit from said relationship.

For me, though, time became my friend, a companion I used to help me get through each day. I wrote a timetable in the diary, highlighting the times when I could sit and take notes, as well as the rest of my responsibilities. I started keeping countdowns of both minor and major events, from birthdays to school days left in a term. It felt like time itself had become a driving force in my life, giving it structure and direction.

That first time at St. Agnes stretched out to almost two years before a willing family finally brought me into their home. To tell you the truth, I had actually given up all hope of ever finding another home outside of the place after watching countless others come and go from there. Even Sarah left a few months after I lost Heather, and while we had a kind of on-again-off-again friendship, it did sting when I saw her walk out of St. Agnes with a suitcase in hand.

Some people tend to think that friendships come easily to children, especially to those caught in precarious situations and craving any sort of companionship on account of the loneliness and lack of love. I'm here to tell you that this idea couldn't be further from the truth. If you have never been caught in this kind of situation yourself, then I doubt you would fully understand what it means to be alone, and I mean *truly* alone.

To me, loneliness isn't how you might view it. To you, loneliness probably means you have nobody to talk to, nobody to share games with, or somebody to go on outings with, visiting movie theatres and whatnot. You find loneliness strangely odd, like some unwanted pair of jeans you'd rather swap for the alternative. Not me.

To me, loneliness is solitude, a place I go where I don't have to worry about anybody else's opinion, where my own plans don't matter to anybody else. Being alone isn't a negative, but rather a positive. It's time where I can spend doing the things others might not want to do. Perhaps the most important thing about loneliness for me is security. Just having that space between me and everybody else is enough to ease my mind, to know that my things are safe and I don't have to constantly watch my back. Yes, loneliness for me is where I find peace.

It wasn't always that way, though, not in the beginning, anyway. At first, that loneliness felt like a curse, especially at school. Every time I walked into a class, it felt like the entire room was watching me. It became so bad that at times, I wanted to run and hide, to find somewhere safe like a stall in the toilets, or out behind the maintenance shed. I figured that if the others couldn't see me, then they wouldn't think about me. It wasn't as if I was at the forefront of everybody's mind.

But as the days and weeks began to pass, I found it so much easier to be alone. I lived in my own little world and only came out at select times, like when asked to read something out loud in the classroom. I pushed through moments like that, knowing that the sooner I started, the sooner I finished and could sit down again. I found myself constantly volunteering to be the first at most things in class, just to get it over with. It wasn't until that certain Tuesday in late June of 1996, a couple of months after my tenth birthday, that I finally found a reason to smile again. That was the day Joy and George Becker walked into my life.

The Beckers weren't what I'd class as ordinary folks. Aged somewhere in their mid-fifties, the couple had never been blessed with children, or so they told me. They said that God had chosen for them to continue their work as missionaries somewhere in East Africa, a place they had spent the majority of the previous twenty-something years. George had been a civil engineer by trade and had worked on quite a number of projects while in those southern lands. Always one to stand by her husband, Joy had worked with some of the local churches and had helped with her brand of building.

By the mid-nineties, both George and Joy decided that it was time to return to England and had begun the process of adopting a local girl which they were to bring back to their own country, however the local authorities blocked the venture when the child's relatives demanded large sums of money for the girl, something the Beckers were advised by their lawyer not to go through with. Or so they told me.

Instead, the couple returned home and after spending a couple of months working out whether they truly wanted a child, they decided to adopt one a lot closer to home and ended up choosing a ten-year-old girl from St. Agnes, a girl who was only too happy to finally leave a place she considered her own private hell. If only things had played out differently.

Fate has a funny way of showing up sometimes. I know of particular moments where I would have given anything for fate to intervene and send me down a specific path, and other times where I would have preferred randomness to step in and play. Take that first month with the Beckers. The home felt amazingly warm, with my new adoptive parents always ready to make me feel wanted and special.

They gave me a room fit for a queen, with a four-poster bed and all the beautiful white silk curtains flowing down over the ends. A bunch of fairy lights had been woven through them, and they put out this glow that looked like a warm hug. Rows and rows of soft toys sat on every surface, with teddies and dolls stacked high across the bed, wardrobe, and dressing table. I'd sit there brushing my hair and wonder how I ever became so lucky.

I lived in that home for three weeks, four days, and eleven hours exactly, just enough time to wonder whether a girl like me had finally been granted a wish I didn't know I had made. Joy had even started teaching me things around her kitchen, with me spending time helping prepare and even cook some of the meals. I felt a part of something, a real member of a family, even if I was the only child and the two grown-ups clearly weren't my parents. It didn't seem to matter. We found our place in the universe, each of us contributing to something special.

What I didn't know was that the couple I had considered calling mum and dad were actually part of a sophisticated group of pedophiles and had been secretly filming me via various forms throughout the house. The mirror on my dressing table was a *two-way* mirror. A secret room sat immediately next to my bedroom, and a camera had been set up to film everything. The same with the mirror in the bathroom, which was located on the other side of the hallway cupboard. The cupboard had a fake back wall, and when opened, it revealed a secret room explicitly designed for spying and filming on whoever happened to be using the two rooms.

I found out the truth in the years that followed after going back and doing some of my own investigation. It wasn't as if the police that eventually raided the house were ever going to share the details with a ten-year-old. They came unannounced on a Saturday morning, seven men and three women bursting through the front door after it imploded from some guy bashing a battering ram against it. I remember screaming when I heard the timber splintering from the impact, and people yelling something about a search warrant. Too many voices yelling at once made it hard to differentiate between them. What I do remember clearly, however, was George's words as he looked at his wife with wide eyes.

"Oh shit," was what he said, and he immediately turned to face away from the door with his hands tucked on top of his head.

At the time, I didn't have a clue about what had been going on and so sat in the kitchen, confused as the officers placed my would-be parents into handcuffs. One of the female officers reassured me that everything would be OK and kept asking if I had been hurt in any way. I obviously shook my head, unaware that I had been just days away from starring in a movie not destined for mainstream cinema.

I don't know what would have happened to me if the Beckers had managed to have their way with me, but what I do know is that it wouldn't have been a pleasant ending. You see, they didn't just face child exploitation charges, plus numerous more for filming me showering, bathing, using the toilet, getting dressed and undressed in my room, plus various other scenes. The Beckers also faced three murder charges back in Zambia, where the bodies of three young girls missing for more than two years had been found buried under the couple's most recent home, located in Lusaka. Interpol had also linked significant pornographic footage featuring the missing girls, as well as numerous others.

I have no doubt that I dodged a proverbial bullet that day, although it was probably best I didn't know it at the time. The plans the couple had for me weren't exactly long-term, which meant that I was extremely lucky not to have been physically harmed. And while I was sad to return to St. Agnes after such a short break from the place, in a way, I should have appreciated the chance to return at all.

CHAPTER 10

The next couple of years passed by with relative ease for me. With the truth about my previous foster parents hidden behind a couple of court orders, and me too young to really understand that stuff anyway, I quickly pulled back into my previous shell, returning to a way of life that felt more homely than anything before. I didn't need friends, and because of that, life became this mundane cycle of school, sleep, and home for me.

It was my adoption by Louise and Henry Fawkner that eventually broke the cycle, despite the couple already having the six-year-old twin girls I mentioned earlier, Eve and Dawn. They told me it wasn't just about having another child in the house, but instead a lot to do with Henry growing up in the system and wanting to help make a difference. He made a difference, alright, although it was not the kind of difference that made things better.

Henry had a way of keeping his abuse secret from his wife. If he were confronting me about some issue, he'd painfully squeeze my shoulder while talking to me, sure to keep his voice down so as not to arouse suspicion. He'd also be constantly watching me, sometimes from a distance and frequently when in the same room. Again, he kept his interest well hidden from his wife.

While Henry's form of discipline had been relatively calm in the beginning, it gradually became more and more physical as time went by. On the day when I first met Jack, I had been in the park reading a book because I needed to get out of the house after a significant argument. I had been using the bathroom, and when I suddenly opened the door to go fetch a towel, I found Henry standing there with his ear pressed against the door. I caught him completely off guard, as evidenced by the fierce colour rising in his cheeks.

He tried to blame me, of course, saying that he was just checking if the room was empty so he could go in, but I pointed out that people usually knock when trying to determine a vacant room. His slap connected with my cheek like a gunshot, and the surprise on his face hinted that his hand reacted long before his brain did. The bruise blossomed almost immediately, and while he tried to apologise, I wasn't going to hang around listening to it. Instead, I grabbed the first book I could find after getting dressed and rushed from the house. I did hear Louise call after me from the living room, but the front door slamming closed cut her words off.

Normally, I would have never allowed myself to interact with someone when in such a mood, but sitting there alone in the park, I think I just needed someone to talk to. I'd met Ollie the previous day, of course, but that had been a much better day, and I was only cutting through the park on my way home from the corner shop. The day I met Jack had played out so differently, with the lead-up to us meeting feeling like something pulling me towards the park.

Just so you know, I'm not going to go over old ground here with you. You've already read about that first meeting in detail, and while I could give you my point of view, I really don't see the point of painting an irrelevant moment from two different angles. You've been through it once already, and there are far more important matters for me to share with you.

Do you remember the summer I spent with the boys down at Bexhall and the whole beach thing? That would never have happened if Louise hadn't walked in on Henry giving me another one of those shoulder-squeezing pep talks he liked to give, the kind where it was just me and him in a room and his hand firmly hanging onto me with his voice low to ensure privacy. He let go the second Louise walked in, of course, pushing me away as if his proximity to me somehow embarrassed him. I had asked the two of them about letting me go with Jack and Ollie to Bexhall earlier in the day, and while Louise did say they would think about it at the time, she gave me the OK after walking in on us.

It's not the trip I wanted to share with you. It is, of course, another experience Jack went into detail about in his telling of our story and not one I can really offer anything new about. One of the moments I do want to share with you, however, happened not long after we returned from that incredible adventure. I sometimes wonder whether the trip to Bexhall had been the universe giving us one last moment of pure childhood bliss before dragging us back and throwing us into the grown-up pile where we finally discovered the real meaning of reality.

Do you recall the argument between Jack and Ollie when one accused the other of liking me a little more than just an innocent friendship, and Jack watched Ollie smoking a joint? Ollie had been smoking cigarettes for quite some time before that day, and while we tried to talk him out of doing it, our advice fell on deaf ears. Jack and I went around to Ollie's house after he had spent all that time with his aunt and found most of his home's contents out on the front lawn as they were expecting an inheritance to come through.

Jack and I had spent the majority of that Sunday playing Mario kart in his bedroom, but during the early afternoon, we began to talk more and more about Ollie and his mental state. We both knew he needed help and so we decided to go around to his house together to see how he was doing. It was evident from the very beginning that Ollie wasn't in the best state of mind during that visit, and I ended up insisting that he come home with me. That much you already know.

What you don't know is what happened during that visit back

to my place. The thing is, Jack didn't know it at the time, and neither did Ollie, but the reason I wanted one of them to come home with me was because I was scared to go back on my own. Henry had begun drinking much more heavily than usual, and his fights with Louise had also significantly increased in volatility. He wasn't just taking his anger out on his wife, but also on his twins and me.

We were almost back to my place when I stopped and reconsidered the idea. There was no way that Henry or Louise would let a boy stay with me at the house, let alone in my room, and so I made up a lie about us needing to hang out in the playroom at the bottom of the garden. Ollie didn't seem to mind and even snuck into the yard behind me when I led him through the side gate and along the hedge.

We hung out for an hour or so before I had to go back inside, but I promised to sneak out of the house again to bring him some food after dinner. Ollie said he was happy just to lie on the bean bag and sleep, and that's precisely how I found him a couple of hours later when I snuck him out some of the leftovers from our meal. He barely chewed the food, finishing the Shepherd's Pie in three or four bites, and washing it down with the chocolate milk.

"I wish I could have brought more, but there wasn't a lot to begin with," I said once he swallowed the last bit of it.

"That was amazing," Ollie said. "Your mum is an incredible cook."

"She's not my mum, Ollie."

"No, of course not," Ollie said with a hint of embarrassment.

"Just saying that she's a great cook."

"That she is."

We didn't talk for long as I had to go back inside, but I did sneak out again about an hour after I told Henry and Louise that I was going to bed. I had begun locking my bedroom door a few weeks earlier after finding Henry going through my drawers one day, and Louise didn't seem to mind me doing so, which I put down to her knowing something about her husband that she didn't want anybody else knowing. Maybe she just knew a girl my age needed privacy, and so I used the locked door to my advantage.

With the door locked and my bedroom lights turned off, I climbed out of the window and visited Ollie for the third time that night. He wasn't sleeping, but he did have the beanbag out behind the shed where he wouldn't be seen. He was lying there on his back smoking what I thought was a cigarette, one arm across his forehead as he stared up at the night sky. I watched him from the corner of the shed for a minute or so, wondering whether either of our lives would ever get better.

When I finally walked over to him, he moved over a bit and gestured for me to lie next to him. I did, curling up next to my friend for a bit of comfort and warmth. We weren't interested in anything more, or at least I wasn't. I don't think Ollie was either, because he had never mentioned it, not then, and not in the years following. We were simply two friends hanging out, watching the stars and comforted by the other's presence.

With neither of us wearing a watch, I'm not sure how long we lay out there before the clouds began to roll in, effectively killing our view. We headed into the playroom, where I sat cross-legged on the floor in front of the small heater Henry had set up for the kids. It didn't exactly have a lot of output, but it could change the ambient temperature in the room if given enough time. I didn't care. Even the slightest warmth was enough for me. Ollie sat with his back pressed up against the wall to the side, and the second he took his seat, he began to roll a fresh joint.

"Why do you smoke so much?" I asked. The concept still hadn't really made sense to my thirteen-year-old brain, and to me, Ollie just appeared so much more mature than I was. He even felt years ahead of Jack, who happened to be the same age.

"It helps me relax," was what he said after lighting it up and taking a deep drag that he held in for a few seconds. And that's when it happened, one of those moments in time where you can look back on and say, *Yup, that's the moment right there.*

"Try it," Ollie said as he held the joint out to me.

A thousand thoughts hit me all at once, each a different viewpoint and opinion of the same offer. The right side of my brain immediately began to debate with the left side, the good girl arguing with the bad. It felt like I stood on the very precipice of fate itself, the decision one I would either appreciate or regret in an instant.

"It won't bite," Ollie said as he leaned a little closer, trying to stretch his arm out enough for me to be able to reach the smoke. He watched me, our eyes meeting as he was searching for the apprehension within me so he could will it away.

I don't know why I did it, but the whole thing happened so fast that I'm not even sure I was part of the final decision at all. One second I was staring at the upheld hand dangling the joint in front of me, the next I was handing it back and feeling a kind of warmth inside my chest. I wanted to cough, the weird plant-like taste in my mouth feeling obnoxiously foreign, but I resisted the urge. I didn't want Ollie laughing at me, and I certainly didn't want him thinking that I might have been too immature for such activities. One of the most pressing emotions when dealing with peer group pressure as a kid is being thought of as a kid.

The effects from that first drag didn't hit me immediately, although I do remember the beating in my chest feeling a lot more uncomfortable than it had during other nervous moments. Ollie watched me with a kind of expectation, a wry grin waiting for a punch line that he could laugh at. He expected me to cough, that much was clear, but I think he was also waiting for me to react to the effects of the smoke.

When that bubble hit me, I felt myself floating down to the ground on a pillow, this weird tingle engulfing my entire existence. I couldn't decide which of the effects I favoured most, with a sense of calmness washing over me like a cloud of inner peace. I lost track of Ollie when I closed my eyes and let myself fall down, my head relaxing on the edge of the beanbag.

"How are you feeling?" Ollie asked. "Want another drag?"

I did, of course, and after sharing the entire joint, I climbed back in through the bedroom, where I lay on the bed for almost the entire night, not knowing whether I could ever sleep again. It had been my first introduction to drugs, and I actually couldn't understand why Jack and everybody else had judged Ollie so badly for it. What I didn't know was that it wouldn't be long until I discovered the reason, one not even my closest friends could save me from.

The joint became something of a secret between Ollie and me. We both agreed to keep the night to ourselves, and I appreciated him saving me a whole lot of explaining. God knows what would have happened if Jack had found out I had fallen into the drug trap the way Ollie had. It also meant that Jack came to me whenever he wanted to vent about Ollie, and I preferred to keep our issues within our tight little circle.

The other moment I wanted to share with you, which you may not have read about yet, is the time when Jack came and stayed with me and my family after his foster mother had the stroke. It hadn't been easy for any of them, given how close the family had been, but I think Jack struggled the most because of how he felt betrayed, not because of the stroke itself, but because of how Roger reacted. He'd basically cut Jack off with a single look, one tiny moment where the man let his guard down enough to reveal his true feelings about the boy.

I think those must have been two of the toughest weeks for Jack. He only ever came right and said how he truly felt one night when we sat in the playroom alone on a Sunday afternoon. Henry had gone on a fishing trip with buddies, and Louise had asked whether we wanted to help the girls with some painting out in the playroom. We spent almost two hours colouring in dozens of pictures before the two of them fell asleep on the beanbag, leaving Jack and me alone to talk in private.

"How am I supposed to trust anybody again?" he asked in frustration when I asked why he didn't want to go back to the home.

"But they love you," I told him, not a lie since I had been to the house plenty of times myself. "They want you there."

"No, they don't, Em," he told me. "Or at least Roger doesn't. If you could have seen what I saw that day, you would understand. He…the way he looked at me…the way he glared at me with such contempt." Jack should shake his head with disappointment. "I may not be the sharpest tool in the shed, but I know enough to understand what that look meant."

"What do you think is going to happen?"

"I don't know," he said, but I could tell that he had an idea, we both did. System kids, or the rag brigade, if you will, always do. We understand how the world works, especially when it comes to kids our age. We're not old enough to be thrown out onto the street, and that meant only one thing.

Louise had insisted on the twins sharing a room while Jack was there, and so Henry had put a second mattress on the floor of Eve's room. He appreciated the gesture, of course, constantly thanking the couple for helping him. It added yet another level of respect for him, one that I couldn't quite understand, given how I had viewed people before him. Manners weren't exactly a common thing amongst those I had grown up with, especially young, angry boys, but Jack seemed to use those manners as a way of keeping himself normal, if that makes sense.

It was during that afternoon of hanging out in the playroom that Jack came clean about his fears of getting sent back to Whispering Hall, and it had nothing to do with the people there. Maybe it was because of my own time at St. Agnes that I understood exactly what he meant without him saying a single word on the subject. It was one of those things we simply understood about each other because of the time we spent in the system.

Unlike me, Jack didn't see loneliness as a good thing; in fact, he feared it, maybe more so than any other thing and the reason why is simple. Loneliness reminded him of abandonment, as it did for many kids who end up in the system, regardless of the country they are in. I believe that abandonment lies at the root cause of more depression and fear for kids than any other emotion.

It took Jack a few days to get comfortable enough to share, but once he did, I got to know a completely different person from the one I thought I had been friends with. The person who opened up to me revealed the harsh realities of his existence, his fears, and some of his most profound and darkest secrets. He shared the murder of a foster father, the loss of friends, and his fear of losing more if he got too close to people. I felt a connection with him, unlike any I had ever experienced, perhaps even deeper than the one I had with Heather.

We shared so much during that year, and in a way, it was those connections that would eventually help each of us with our own personal struggles once life pulled us in different directions. I know for me personally, I would never have made it through if I didn't have the support of my friends, the best friends I could ever ask for.

CHAPTER 11

Life continued passing by, with all three of us eventually finding ourselves caught up within the whirlwind of maturity, where grown-up kids needed to deal with grown-up problems. Ollie lost his carer to suicide and then faced issues with his aunt, while Jack lost his own home due to his foster mother suffering a stroke and his foster father no longer being in a position to care for him. Jack ended up returning to Whispering Hall, while Ollie moved on as well after his aunt ended up in detox. As for me? I decided to make the most out of a bad situation.

Two weeks after my fourteenth birthday, I found myself walking around Newham, an area on the east side of London. It's not a place I knew well, but considering it was where my mother lived before she died, you could say that I had somewhat of an interest in the place. I walked past the building where my grandmother still lived, and eventually found myself talking to one of my aunts while sitting on the fence of her front yard.

Out of all of my known relatives, Elisa was the only one I could ever talk to, and even that was a struggle. She spoke with an air of arrogance, as if she were better than me, almost gloating about how her own mother would never have given up her children, no matter what. She talked as if my mother had been the worst woman in the world, and that I deserved so much better.

"You could always come and stay here, if you want," she told me while sipping on a can of beer at eleven in the morning. She had four kids herself, the youngest around my age and all of them still living with her. "I'd have to ask Brett, but he'd be OK with it." Brett was her boyfriend and not one of the four fathers of her kids, which should explain things enough for you.

Despite her being family, to a certain extent, I couldn't do it, and I know the system favoured my decision on the matter. The broken windows and dishevelled front yard were evidence enough of the problematic life these people lived. Her two eldest sons both sat in jail for armed robbery, while one of her daughters was already pregnant with her second child at seventeen. Elisa's fourteen-year-old daughter had recently suffered a miscarriage, and when the girl walked out of the door to ask her mother something, Elisa playfully slapped her butt while laughing and said, "Maybe now you'll take more care about who you let stick things into you."

The whole thing was a joke to her, sad but true. I wasn't even sure why I had bothered going there at all, since I'd always struggled so much the previous times, which numbered exactly two. Maybe it was my own need for feeling wanted that drove me to visit with them, or maybe it was just to give myself a reminder of the kind of life I wanted to avoid. This time, however, Elisa said something that changed everything.

"Ray is back in town," she told me once her daughter walked back inside, the girl pretending to limp as if her miscarriage somehow injured her foot.

Hearing the name sent weird phantom fingers into my stomach; the tightening feeling was uncomfortable as I looked at her. Elisa saw my expression change and grinned.

"He's living not far from here. You've met your father, haven't you?"

I nodded, but that was just to acknowledge her question, a large part of me unsure of whether I wanted to acknowledge the name at all. I had only met my father once before, and his reaction is something I will never forget, nor the words he spoke once he found out who I was.

"I got no money to give you," was his reply to my telling him that I was Megan Grant's daughter.

He didn't even look at me at first; the man simply shrugged his shoulders as he focused on his latest high. I remember his pupils being just pinpricks, something I recognised as him using heroin, compared to other drugs. The man had been an addict for as long as I had known him to be a part of my life, a very *insignificant* amount of time in my life. Let's face it, a guy volunteering some sperm almost fifteen years earlier doesn't automatically give them fatherhood status, but I was curious about who he was. Who wouldn't be?

Our first meeting lasted about fifteen seconds, I assume around the same length of time he took to inject my mother with the stuff that resulted in me. OK, call it a low blow, but I don't have much more than insults to throw at a guy who has never made the slightest effort to better himself in life. The man shrugged me off like a bad deal that first time, and the second time didn't fare much better. That time, I had managed to catch him sitting at a bus stop and spoke to him for about a minute before his ride came along and whisked him away again. He told me that I looked so much like my mother and that he wished he could have built a life with her. He said pretty much all the things one would when trying to make it sound like they were paying attention, but didn't have much input. He looked uncomfortable with me there and almost relieved when he pointed to his bus and stood.

"We'll have to catch up sometime and sit down and talk," was what he told me just before boarding the bus, his retreat looking more like an escape. I could see the relief on his face when I didn't say anything about him leaving. I simply watched him board the bus, the door closed as he walked down the aisle to the nearest seat, and then the bus continued down the road with me standing alone by the roadside, wondering if I had made a mistake trying to find him.

Two visits, and both combined lasted less than five minutes. Ray Burrows wasn't exactly a talkative guy when it came to his own flesh and blood. Most of the questions I had carried with me for most of my life were answered within thirty seconds with no words needed, but a few remained, a few that I needed to save for a better time if I wanted them answered.

It didn't come as much of a surprise when Elisa said she had some urgent business to take care of. She had emptied her beer a few minutes earlier, and with a couple of kids arguing inside her home, she used the opportunity to wish me well and to drop by whenever I wanted to. I know she was just being polite. She was one of the few people in our family who still possessed a mild sense of manners. I did thank her for chatting with me, but truth be told, I felt somewhat relieved to get out of there. Being around any of my own family members made me nervous.

I walked for the next two and a half blocks without seeing any of the traffic or buildings I passed, my brain too preoccupied with trying to work out whether to go and see my father. A part of me wanted to, of course, but another part kept telling me not to bother, that I had already given the man enough chances to at least try to get to know me. It wasn't as if he had anything I wanted. As far as I was concerned, his commitment to me as a parent ended the day he walked out on my mother shortly before my birth.

As it turned out, I didn't have to go quite as far as Elisa had told me. I was still at least three blocks from the address she gave me for him when I found Ray Burrows sitting on a park bench with the top of a brown bottle sticking out of the top of a brown paper bag wedged between his legs. He sat upright, a pair of sunglasses hiding his eyes and a baseball cap shadowing the rest of his face, but I knew it was him. The scar on his left cheek couldn't be hidden, and neither could the mass of red curls poking out from under the cap.

I didn't walk right up to him at first. Instead, I walked to another bench that sat about thirty metres behind him and to the left. From there, I saw a kind of side profile of him and watched as he took random swigs from the bottle while mouthing something to himself. He didn't seem to pay attention to anybody walking by, but he did take a keen interest in a woman walking her dog. He chuckled to himself when she stopped to bag up her dog's crap, and I heard him whistle as she bent over.

Something about seeing Ray like that made me feel sorry for him. I don't know why, since I didn't exactly have a history with the guy, but I guess it has something to do with my own humanity. Hate isn't a word I have ever felt comfortable using, which might surprise you, but to me, hatred speaks more about the person feeling it than the person at the other end. It's not a word I throw around willy nilly, and Ray didn't fit the mould for its use.

I'm not sure how long I sat there watching him before I finally got off the bench and walked towards him. I also didn't know how cooked he was, from the alcohol or possible drugs, since I hadn't seen him enter the park. When he looked in my direction, I saw something in his face immediately change, and not just from the recognition. He looked...ashamed, in a way, as if seeing me reminded him of something he wasn't quite ready to face.

"Look who it is," I heard him mumble under his breath before he took another swig. He waited until I got a bit closer before adding, "Didn't catch me at a good time, oh child of mine."

"I'm not here to judge you, Ray," I said and sat on the other end of the bench. It was the first time I had called him by his first name, and he looked at me weirdly. Actually, it was the first time I called him anything.

We sat in silence for maybe a couple of minutes, with me watching the traffic out on the road and Ray staring at the dirt between his worn runners. I think we both tried to feel the situation for what it was, each of us unsure of how to proceed. For Ray, I think the hardest thing was knowing he had never been anything of a father figure to me, and since he had no other children that he knew of, that left me as his only offspring, of sorts. Maybe that's why he felt a need to start the conversation, and when he started talking, it was the last thing I expected to hear from him.

"I didn't walk out on her, you know?"

"Who?" I asked, at first caught off guard by his words. I actually thought he forgot who had sat down next to him, maybe the alcohol affecting his awareness, but then when he took his sunglasses off and looked at me, I could see there was no confusion.

"I loved Meg, I really did," he said as he folded the arm of his glasses and tucked them to the top of his t-shirt. "She had this…this incredible smile when she was happy. I always saw a kind of twinkle in her eye that I was sure was only meant for me." He chuckled once, briefly, and I watched his lips purse tightly.

"I don't really remember her talking about you," I said, not sure what to say but positive that I wanted to hear more. I wanted to keep the conversation going, but wasn't sure how. It wasn't as if I knew anything about either one of them other than what I'd been told by my aunt.

"It might surprise you to know that I've often gone down to where they found Meg," he said as he dipped his eyes, perhaps shame getting the better of him. I think I saw a hint of colour briefly flare up in his cheeks, but I couldn't be sure given the poor complexion of his skin and the volume of alcohol in his system.

"I don't know where that is," I said, feeling somewhat relieved at being able to drop at least one truthful comment.

Surprisingly, Ray told me an address and even offered to write it down for me when I said I didn't have a mobile phone.

"Just walk to the end of the street, and there's this little laneway that takes you down to the river's edge. You can also continue along the main road and then jump the barrier, but it's much harder to get to the water from there." Surprisingly, he pulled out a piece of paper and a pen and began drawing a little diagram. He shuffled a little closer to show me the primitive map. "Right there next to that tree is where they pulled her body from the water." I saw his bottom lip quiver just a bit before he regained control over his emotions.

"We could go together," I said, not sure if the idea was a good one. I actually surprised myself, the words rolling off my tongue before I had a chance to consider them.

"Yeah, maybe one day," Ray said and gripped the neck of the bottle a little tighter.

The silence between us returned a little too easily, and I ended up thanking Ray before making my escape. I'm not sure why I felt a need to, but I held out my hand just before leaving, and he absently shook with me, a couple of strangers signing off with a formal handshake. I ended up finding the nearest bus stop about half a block further up, and when the bus drove past the park some twenty minutes later, my father was gone. If I had known it would be the last time I saw him, I might have tried a little bit harder, but fate rarely gives notice.

Ray Burrows died two days later after walking out of a pub drunk shortly before midnight and getting hit by a taxi. The force of the impact sent him skittering along the road right into the path of an oncoming police car. They say he died long before the second car hit him. As for me, I ended up going down to the spot where he guided me with the map, and after walking up and down the narrow patch of grass, I found a small marker with my mother's initials.

I don't know whether he meant for me to find the other sign he had left, a small carving on an adjacent tree that read R.B. 4 M.G. He had encircled the message with a loveheart that had faded somewhat with the passage of time, but it remained mostly legible. In a comforting kind of way, I saw it as his way of showing that he wasn't just some drunk loser I always imagined him to be. He had problems, demons in his head like we all do and in a way, that gave him more humanity than most people I knew.

CHAPTER 12

I sometimes see that final day beside the river, finding the moniker from my father to my mother as a kind of gateway, the last real day of my independence, my childhood. That was the final day when I stopped feeling reliant on the grown-ups around me and knew that I would eventually need to take care of myself if I was going to have any chance in this world. Growing up is easy when you have all the necessary tools explained to you, but growing up in a system that felt more like a production line, wanting to get you to the other end as quickly as possible to make way for a new batch, came with its own bunch of challenges.

If you think that life continued on like a fairytale for me, then you're sadly mistaken, because I've only been warming up. I guess I did have it a lot easier than many of my fellow rag brigaders, but reality was never going to continue passing me by. I don't know whether I ever openly blamed Henry and Louise for what happened next, but I do know that if things hadn't played out the way they had, I could have avoided the rest of the nightmare that quickly followed.

The issues began the very next day after finding the place where my mother had been found dead, floating in the river, after a client strangled her and dumped the body into the water. You can imagine how surreal it all felt for me, to sit in the very same place where my own mother had lain all those years earlier. To think that she had been in the very same place, with nobody there to help her.

I don't think I slept at all that night, which was why I heard someone trying to get into my room in the very early hours of the morning. I'm talking like two or three. The door handle kept twisting slowly back and forth, but with me having locked it right before I went to bed, the door remained shut. A small gap underneath the bottom edge showed just enough of a reflection in the floor tiles for me to recognise Henry's pyjama bottoms and the butterflies in my stomach just about exploded with fear.

It was during breakfast the next morning that the fireworks really took off. I wasn't sure how to approach the subject and with Henry and Louise already in the middle of some sort of argument, my addition was never going to make things end well.

"How did you sleep?" Louise asked me as she set two kinds of cereal down on the table. The twins each grabbed a box, leaving me waiting for them to finish pouring their own.

"OK, until someone woke me around three," I said and nodded at Eve for the Frosties.

"Why, what happened? Bad dream?"

"No, someone was trying to get into my room," I said, trying my hardest to sound nonchalant about it. While I didn't look directly at him, I saw Henry shift uncomfortably in his chair while drinking his coffee.

"What do you mean, sweetie?" Louise asked. "We were all sleeping." She looked at each of the twins, thinking it might have been one of them. It was when I looked at Henry for a brief glimpse and then back at my bowl that Louise picked up on it.

"Henry?"

I don't think Louise meant to accuse him. I actually think she just said the name because I looked at him, maybe asking herself whether it could have been him. Unfortunately, guilty minds don't tend to react in a sane manner, and hearing his name, Henry just about flipped out.

"I wasn't trying to do anything," he snapped angrily. "Got the doors confused, that's all."

"Doors confused how?" Louise asked with her hands held out. With the animosity already at fever pitch, it didn't take much to set each of them off.

"I thought it was the bathroom. I needed a piss, and…"

"You what? Henry, you piece of shit, I told you before that this isn't -"

"Shut the hell up," Henry yelled at Louise and before I knew it, the guncrack of a slap echoed through the kitchen. Eve yelled out in shock, Dawn slid off her chair and slid under the table to hide, and I sat there with a spoon held out in front of me as if I was ready to defend myself at all costs.

Not content with hitting his wife, Henry charged at me, easily sidestepped the spoon when I threw it at him, and grabbed me by the hair. When Louise lunged at him to try and stop his attack, he struck her square in the face with a punch that I immediately assumed broke her nose. I screamed as he tightened his fingers into my hair, the pain feeling like heat, and when he pulled me out of the chair, I thought my scalp would surely tear itself free from my head.

"You want to accuse me of shit like that, little lady, you can just go and find yourself another home," he screamed while dragging me towards the hallway and eventually into my room. Once through the doorway, he easily picked me up and tossed me onto the floor, before going to the wardrobe where he pulled a suitcase down from the top of it.

"Pack your shit," he yelled, threw the suitcase onto the floor beside me and left the room.

I heard more shouting from the kitchen, as well as the girls crying uncontrollably. I watched Dawn come into the hallway and run towards her room and she completely ignored me when I tried to call out to her. Louise came next, holding Eve close as Henry followed them while screaming abuse at them. He looked like a man completely unhinged, his temper, which he had controlled well during my time there, now on the loose.

While I expected the police to attend, they never showed up. I guess the neighbours didn't consider all the screaming as police worthy and hadn't bothered calling anybody for help. I think one of the neighbours did show up, but I couldn't be sure, as Henry answered the door and then stepped outside onto the porch with whoever it was.

As for Louise, she eventually came and saw me, closed the door and sat me down on the bed. The house had been quiet for a couple of hours, with each of the girls in their respective rooms with the doors closed, and Henry and Louise in their own room. There had been no yelling, no arguing of any kind, and at one point, I wondered whether he had actually followed through and killed her, maybe all three of his family.

"I wish I could make it work, kiddo," she told me without actually looking at me. "But I think you know why I need you to go."

I could see the guilt in her eyes when she finally met my gaze and the sad truth is, that I don't blame her at all. I think what Louise wanted to tell me and what she ended up saying were two truths miles apart. Somehow, without hearing her real words, I knew that she wanted to save me. I think she knew that Henry had tried to come in my room, and perhaps that hadn't been the first time. I think she understood the danger I was in and she wanted to help me escape.

When I left the house that afternoon in the company of a social worker, I did so without ever looking back. Not when I walked to the car and not when that car drove me away for the last time. What I understood more clearly than anything was that I had never been a part of that family. They could pretend as much as they wanted to, but the cold hard truth remained. They had their family before I came along, and I was nothing more than a glorified guest, someone to make themselves feel better about themselves by appearing to openly welcome someone in need into their home.

No other existence had ever made me feel more a part of the rag brigade than the Fawkners did. It was because of them and the events of that day that ended up sending me down a completely different path, one that I couldn't have imagined just a few weeks earlier. With a single temper tantrum, Henry managed to change the course of not only my life, but also his own. Louise ended up kicking him out just four weeks later and eventually filed the paperwork for divorce.

Sandra Beatty was the woman who picked me up from the Fawkner residence, and with no vacancies at St. Agnes, she took me to the next best option within the area, which was this halfway house a couple of suburbs over. Lord's wasn't exactly a supervised home for children like St. Agnes, but more so a place built for teens and young adults. Sandra told me that the age range of the girls was between thirteen and nineteen, with the older girls at the lower end of the IQ band, if that makes sense.

From the outside, the place looked hands-down like a jail, the bars on all of the windows adding just the right amount of decoration. Inside the foyer, the reception desk followed the same design pattern, with a clear perspex window separating visitors from the reception staff. A harsh-looking woman greeted us with a frown when Sandra walked me inside, and after spending five minutes convincing the woman that I had indeed been assigned to the third-floor common room, a guard finally came to escort us up the stairs.

"Look, I know Blackrock is not the nicest place, but I promise I'll try and get you back into St. Agnes as quickly as possible," Sandra told me on our walk to the third floor. I think she meant it. I could hear the genuine concern in her voice, and during the drive to the home, she did share with me a few pointers about how to keep safe while there.

When we reached the third-floor hallway, I saw a couple of groups of girls standing intermittently spaced along the walls, each falling silent when we neared them. Sandra offered them a smile, and I heard faint giggling once we passed them. Sandra didn't seem to mind, but I felt shame just for being vaguely associated with those girls.

While I had been assigned to the third-floor common room, my bed sat inside Room B, one of four inside.

"You're in B2," Sandra told me when she opened the door and, after finding it empty, closed it again so we had a brief moment of privacy.

It's not often that I can pinpoint the good times during my years in the system, but I can tell you with confidence that the next ten minutes I still remember to this day. The funny thing is, it wasn't even for anything that special, but that's the funny thing about it. Sandra helped me unpack my suitcase, helped me put some of my clothes on the coat hangers and talked to me while doing so. I remember her telling me how she lived in a very similar home back when she was younger, and how she used books to keep herself sane.

"Sometimes, the easiest way to stay out of trouble is to make sure you're not standing in trouble's way," is what she told me with her usual cheery tone, and it was advice I truly appreciated.

The thing about Sandra is that I felt a real connection with her, maybe because she had already lived a life very similar to my own. She had done her time in the homes, had used books the same way I had, and had even faced several tough families along the way.

"Here, take this and keep it safe," she told me just after we finished unpacking. She held out one of her business cards. "If you ever need anything, you make sure and call me."

"I will," I said, and when that wasn't enough, she made me swear it. "I promise, I will call you," I said, and then, completely out of the blue, she hugged me.

I wanted to walk her back to her car once we were finished, but Sandra insisted on my staying in the room, if only for a few minutes to get myself settled.

"You need time to relax yourself, to give yourself a bit of space and unwind," she said. "Use these few minutes alone just to chill"

Sandra left me alone in that room, closing the door after herself and giving me nothing more than her boot heels clip-clopping on the tiled floor while she walked back to the staircase. I sat on the edge of my bed until they faded out completely, and lay back with my head on the pillow. A few minutes after that, the door opened and in walked three girls, all of whom immediately focused on me. While the door to my childhood had finally closed, the door leading into my adulthood had only just opened, and life was about to get a whole lot more interesting.

What happened next is something that I still remember to this day. The girls first introduced themselves after sitting on their respective beds. Nadine on hers, and Alanah on hers. Sissy and Jo sat on the same one, and when I saw them holding hands, I felt something uncomfortable inside me move. Sissy noticed me looking at them awkwardly and grinned.

"Yes, we are together," she said and gave Jo a sensual kiss right in front of me. Nadine giggled and threw a pillow at the girls.

"Oh, cut it out and stop teasing the girl," she said and turned back to me. "Guessing you're not into girls?"

"No," I said, not really sure what I was answering.

Sex hadn't really been something I knew a lot about. The lessons in school didn't really address any of the questions people needed answers to, and my best friends had been boys who were at that uncomfortable stage in life where the subject of girls seemed to turn them into silent and uncomfortable fence posts. It wasn't as if I could have asked Ollie or Jack about that kind of stuff. The closest female friend I ever had was Heather, and at the time, I hadn't quite reached the maturity level where sex talk was a thing.

I think I just kind of fell between the cracks when the other girls my age learned about those sorts of topics. I'm guessing someone would have had an older sister, and then shared the information with their friends before it kind of flowed downhill to everybody else. Unfortunately, for me, I wasn't a part of a group, and so that downhill flow never really reached me. I hadn't even had my first period yet, another reason why I hadn't felt the need to ask awkward questions.

"So, how old are you?" Nadine asked.

"Turned fourteen a few weeks back."

"Oh? What date?" She sounded hopeful, as if needing our dates to match.

"April 8," I said.

"Ah, I'm April 14."

"Yeah, like so close," Jo mocked, and the others giggled.

"Shut up," Nadine said defensively, but didn't sound angry at all. She turned back to me and smiled, and I found that I felt good vibes coming from her. "We were just about to head up to Barney's. Want to come?"

I had no idea what Barney's was, whether it was a person's home, a shop, or some codename for something else, but the truth is, I didn't care. That feeling of inclusion felt so overpowering that I immediately wondered whether I had been wrong in wanting isolation all of those previous years. It's funny how the mind works, sometimes. I guess I used my solitude as a defence mechanism when I struggled to make friendships. It's much easier to tell yourself you don't need friends when in reality, it's the one thing that would have made all the difference in my life.

CHAPTER 13

Friendships turned out to be the one thing I couldn't do without, not after spending a few weeks with the girls at the house. While officially known as Blackrock, the girls simply called it the Rock, on account of making it shorter. Three floors filled with those down on their luck and struggling through life with all manner of addictions and issues. An adjacent building dubbed B-Tower stood four storeys tall and held similar women, with the only difference being their babies. It had a majority population of expectant mothers, as well as a few who had already given birth. The system normally tried to find those with infants a more permanent place to live, although accommodation wasn't that easy to come by.

The one place where everybody seemed to congregate together was a vacant lot behind Blackrock. A small corner store stood three lots over, and you reached it via this alleyway that I immediately felt uncomfortable walking down, even when surrounded by friends. Addicts sat in dark corners, either enjoying their latest highs or struggling through their latest lows. Rows of cardboard boxes and makeshift shelters sat intermittently amongst the vegetation. A couple of people slept inside one of the cardboard boxes when I first walked down the alley, their legs hanging out the end, intertwined with one another. Nadine warned me not to speak to anybody, not to even look at anyone if they called out, something that happened regularly.

Those first few weeks were eye-opening to say the least. I experienced more life in those twenty to thirty days than I had during the previous fourteen years, with my eyes opened to the kind of existence expected of us. Too many girls fell into the trap of feeling more grown-up by being able to make unsupervised decisions on their own. Don't get me wrong, we had supervisors working in the house with us, two per floor, and always on a twenty-four-hour rotating roster. The problem was that even with two experienced minders per floor, it wasn't anywhere near enough for the sheer number of girls living in the place. We're talking fifty to sixty girls per floor, and many with not only serious issues, but also the worst kind of attitude.

I wish I could tell you that I happened to be the unicorn, the one who shunned the rest and managed to avoid all of the bad stuff. I wish I could tell you that my life wasn't going to follow the same pattern as my mother, my grandmother, and most of my aunties. The reality is that sometimes, those friends who I didn't think I needed in my life turned out to be the very same people I should have avoided at all costs, especially when caught in such vulnerable conditions.

May 17th, 2000, was the date I got my first ever period, and Nadine was right there in the bathroom with me when it came. I remember the shock of seeing the blood in the toilet bowl, but it didn't last long. Nadine grabbed one of the pads from the dispensary for me and spent the next week or so working out how often I needed to change them and so on. I don't really want to go into specific details with you. Any female is going to understand what I went through, and any male doesn't really need to know. Call it a girl thing, OK?

The worst thing that happened was Jo finding out I had my first ever period and subsequently making jokes about it to the others while we were all together, sometimes in the company of boys. Yes, there were boys, although we would catch up with them out in the vacant lot. They weren't allowed inside the building, of course, although there were times when some would sneak inside via fire escapes and such and end up in a room with a girl.

It was during those random times standing around the vacant block that I met Zac. He was taller than most, with long dark hair and brilliant blue eyes. He always hung around the same three guys, one of whom was dating Nadine. I think she secretly hoped that Zac and I would become an item, although I wasn't exactly open to such things, having never had a boyfriend before.

Summer time meant warm evenings and for many of us, sitting around in circles at the vacant lot was how we spent most of those nights. There would always be a fire or two, either burning inside a half-cut barrel or just straight on the ground, with the wood usually coming from some of the fallen tree branches or discarded furniture dumped in adjoining streets. We'd sit around these fires drinking, smoking, and just talking about anything in general, while those in relationships held hands or huddled close together.

It was during one of those evenings when Zac came and sat next to me. He offered me a sip of his beer and when I accepted, he put an arm around me as he watched me drink. I didn't like the taste at first; the bitterness was just way too foreign for me. I needed something sweet, although I didn't say so. What made me drink more was when a weird sensation washed over me, this overwhelming feeling of floating in the air. My head felt much lighter and my body seemed to tingle, which seemed to intensify with each sip.

When Zac finally leaned in and kissed me, the rest of those sitting in our circle began to do that annoying oooooo. I felt Zac grin, trying to ignore them, but all I could do was focus on the touch of his lips. I had never even *held* a boy's hand before, let alone kiss one, and it just felt too nice to ignore. When I felt one of his hands start to work its way from my back to the side of my chest, I pulled away.

I wish I could tell you that I pushed him away, that I wasn't some tramp who was going to jump into bed with the first guy who came along. I wish I could tell you that I had morals, the same ones that allowed me to judge my mother, who fell pregnant in similar circumstances to where I was at that very moment. I wish I could tell you those things, but then I'd be lying.

Zac took my virginity inside one of those cardboard boxes, less than an hour later, and without the use of a condom. I had drunk almost an entire bottle of beer, which hit me hard enough to dull my sense of judgement. I don't remember the pain, nor the pleasure, just this guy lying on top of me and grunting a few times with bad breath. I closed my eyes for most of it because of how he kept staring at me with this weird expression. I remember feeling something wet between my legs, and when he finished, he rolled over, lay on his back, and caught his breath. He asked whether it was good, and when I said yes, he kissed me with that same bad breath that nearly made me gag.

When I followed the girls back to the vacant lot the following afternoon, I saw Zac standing with another group, his arm around a girl I hadn't seen before. When our eyes met, he didn't acknowledge me in the slightest; instead, I watched him lean down and kiss the girl on the lips before continuing to talk to his friends.

I struggled to understand what had happened, and even more when Nadine told me it was nothing more than a one-night stand. She said that she lost her cherry the same way, and when I asked what she meant by cherry, she giggled and explained it to me. Alanah told me she lost hers the same way as well, but she was the one to push the guy away. She said she just wanted to get it over with, so that the next time it would be better, not that I understood what she meant.

Would it come as a complete surprise to you to learn that I fell pregnant that first time? There I was, fourteen years old, spending years judging my mother for getting pregnant with me during some drunken stupor and there I was doing the exact same thing, albeit even younger than she was. Missing my next period was the first sign that something was wrong, and when Nadine convinced me to ask the floor supervisor for a pregnancy test, I confirmed it the very next morning.

No, I didn't cry when I saw that second line slowly appear on the test. I didn't even get angry. The truth is, I was too damn shocked to feel anything. I just sat on the toilet seat, dumbfounded and staring at the line. Nadine kept banging on the door trying to get me to open it, which I did eventually, and then I got to sit there while the three girls stood around me making jokes. The real shock came when Alanah said that I had to tell Zac.

I had never thought about how different my life would be if I fell pregnant and had an actual baby. I think I spent the rest of the day and most of that night just lying on my bed alone, staring up at the ceiling. The rest of the girls went out just like they usually did, but I didn't want to go with them. I couldn't go with them. For one thing, I had no idea what I was going to say to Zac if I saw him. Yes, he was older, but I didn't think that at seventeen, he had the life skills needed to take on the responsibility of a child, not that I knew anything about him.

Lying on that bed, I must have spent hours going from one thought to the next and each time wondering how I got myself into such a situation. I imagined my mother lying next to me on the bed, her voice speaking directly into my brain with that I-told-you-so tone.

"You see? It's not that hard to screw up your life in the blink of an eye, is it?"

"It certainly isn't," I said aloud into the silence of the room. In a way, I wanted my mother to hear those words if she were in the room with me. Who knows, maybe she was.

Pregnant. How could I have been so stupid and so naive? I thought myself so much more controlled, so much more responsible, and yet there I was, given the very first taste of alcohol and immediately on my back, giving it all to some boy I didn't even know. I hated myself in that moment, hated myself in a way that I never thought possible. All I could think of was why I would be so careless and just risk everything for the sake of…what?

That was when a voice spoke to me, a voice from my past and one that I hadn't thought of in a long time.

"Your biggest challenge will come from those closest to you," was what Sister Alice told me back when I was first struggling to understand that new world I had been dropped into. She used the term peer group pressure on more than one occasion, and in my arrogance, I believed I could outsmart it by not keeping friends. How easily I was fooled.

Taking Nadine's advice, I did end up confronting Zac with the news and while I would have preferred to have left that incident in the past, I did promise in the very beginning to be as truthful as possible. I don't think I have ever felt such shame as I did in that moment when it felt like the entire world decided to judge me.

"Pregnant with *my* baby?" Zac first said when he forced me to talk in front of his friends. And that was when he looked at some of the others and grinned. "This chick sleeps with any guy after a few minutes," he said and laughed. "That baby could belong to a dozen other guys, for all I know." He sounded so disrespectful, and when the rest of the group continued laughing, Zac said, "Just get rid of it."

Get rid of it. I couldn't believe I heard him right, but I didn't hang around to ask him to repeat himself. Instead, I turned and ran back to the Rock, desperate to get away from the sound of the laughter. I passed by Nadine and the others who called out to me, but the falling tears and heat in my cheeks were enough of a sign for me to keep going.

I think I sank into a deep depression over the next few days, with me barely leaving the room, except to use the bathroom. The girls even tried bringing me food since I wasn't going to the dining room, but my appetite had dwindled down to nothing. I couldn't eat, I couldn't sleep, and conversation barely went past initial greetings. It was as if I had fallen into a deep, dark hole and didn't know how to get myself out again.

Three weeks after that pregnancy test, I woke up to find the bedsheet covered in blood. At first, I thought I must have peed myself in the middle of the night but when I pulled the blanket back and saw the horror underneath, I just about screamed with terror. Nadine saw my reaction, with her constantly waking up before anyone else, and it was she who took me to the bathroom and helped me clean myself up.

I miscarried the first pregnancy I ever had, the ordeal lasting just a couple of days. The cramping was some of the worst of my life, but I considered it a small price to pay for the chance not to be linked to a guy who used me like a cheap whore and then bragged about it to his friends. I carried his baby for all of six weeks, give or take, and the complexity of the situation seemed to fade away as easily as flushing a toilet.

Someone once asked me what it felt like to lose a baby when I was so young, and my answer is always the same. Judge me or not, but it felt like the best kind of relief. Sure, I would have loved the child if I had gone the whole term, and I would have taken care of it, the way my mother should have with me, but that miscarriage saved me from needing to make those sorts of decisions. It actually saved me from *all* decisions; the entire dilemma washed away in an instant.

CHAPTER 14

While you might think that life got better for me once I lost the baby, the truth is, things became even worse. Sister Alice had been right all those years earlier. Peer group pressure really is a challenging situation to get through, and I'm ashamed to say that I failed more times than just that one pregnancy. The miscarriage was one of two within the space of a year, and it wasn't even the worst thing to happen to me.

The depression didn't go away when I lost the baby, the way I thought it might. In fact, it became so much worse, and I found that the only way I could drag myself out of the hole was by drinking whatever alcohol I could get my hands on. We didn't exactly have much in the way of funds, but we became pretty adept at stealing, especially when the four of us went out together. Some days, we would end up with enough food and drink to put on a party and party we did. Often spending entire nights out in the vacant lot, partying up with friends and strangers and anybody else who walked in. And that was how I came to meet the second vice of my life, a vice that took things to an entirely different level.

Adam was different from all the other boys, or so I thought. He seemed caring, more attentive than the others. Unlike Zac, he didn't try to spike me with alcohol to get me to sleep with him. Instead, he took me to a quieter part of the lot where we sat and cuddled under a blanket while watching what few stars were visible. He really listened to me, and not just in a fake kind of way the way other boys had. He seemed genuinely interested, which is why I believe I fell in love with him.

The first time we slept together, he appeared so nervous, his hands shaking as he tried to remove my bra. I ended up having to help him with the clasp, and then reassured him it was what I really wanted. The sex was great, so different from what I had with Zac. Adam took his time and paid more attention to me, which, let's face it, I wasn't about to complain about. Unfortunately for me, alcohol and sex weren't the only things Adam brought to the table with him.

It happened one night while we were alone in my room. Adam managed to sneak into the building via the back loading dock during a laundry delivery. It wasn't uncommon, given the loading dock's proximity to the fire escape stairwell and with a few well-timed distractions, the girls managed to help sneak several boys in at once. We also split up between the rooms, although sometimes, it wasn't always possible, and so we might end up sharing a room while doing the thing. Beggars can't be choosers, right?

On this particular night, we didn't start off the usual way. Adam had been wound up on account of his brother, and rather than getting down to business, he just kind of sat on the bed with his back pressed up against the wall. He didn't open up at first, but when I pressed him, he admitted that he no longer wanted to stay at his house. He said his mother had a new boyfriend who liked to beat him and his brother up, but it was also his brother who told him not to do anything, as his mother might suffer.

"I just want to get out of there," he said, hitting his leg in frustration.

"Then get out of there," I said, still too young and dumb to fully comprehend what that meant in the real world.

"And go where, Emma?"

That was when he pulled something out of his pocket which at first, I didn't recognize. It was only when he asked me for the lighter I kept in my top drawer that I saw the spoon he held in one hand. I couldn't stop looking at it as I watched Adam slowly move the flame back and forth underneath. The powder quickly melted, and Adam pulled out a syringe, which he used to draw up the liquid.

"I got enough for two if you want some," he said and half held the needle out to me.

There I was, fifteen years old with a guy I deeply cared about and the whole world in front of us. We could have done so much with our lives, but sometimes, it's the decisions we make on the spur of the moment that come back to haunt us the most. None of the peer group pressure I had experienced compared to that moment, and while Adam's question did push me towards the decision, my own curiosity was what pushed me over the edge.

I had seen drugs before, of course. Hell, who wouldn't have in a place like Blackrock House. People literally shot up in some of the hallways, stairwells, bathrooms, and anywhere else they could find. Privacy wasn't really a thing, and the supervisors didn't have the time to patrol all areas at all times. They spent the majority of their time dealing with one-on-one issues in their offices, and the queue outside their offices was usually four or five deep during daytime hours.

But seeing people use drugs and being offered to use them are two completely different things, I can attest to that. While I might have looked down on those who used it initially, it wasn't until someone actually offered me a sample that the rose-coloured glasses came off. All it took was a faint head nod, and Adam turned his attention to me. He removed his belt and tied it around the upper part of my arm before tapping the tender skin of my inner elbow.

"Does it hurt?" I asked.

"Just a pinch," he said and gave my hand a reassuring squeeze before focusing on the needle tip.

I had never been able to watch someone stick a needle into my arm before that night, but something about the mystery around it kept my eyes on it. I felt more nervous than ever before, nervous enough for the beating in my chest to stretch all the way up into my temples, and still I couldn't look away. I watched as the tip of the needle trembled just a bit before I felt its seductive tip touch the delicate skin. Adam looked at me a final time, smiled, and pushed.

He was right. It did pinch at first, but that initial bite of pain barely lasted a second before an icy chill went cascading up my arm. I couldn't look away as he squeezed the plunger slightly down before drawing it back up and pulling neat little droplets of blood into the clear syringe. It mingled with the clear liquid for a few seconds before Adam slowly pushed the rest of it into me.

The rush felt overwhelming, a freight train of cold tingles coursing through my neck, and finally into my brain. It felt like someone had taken my body, flipped it upside down and kept dunking me between a hot and a cold tub of water. I couldn't work out which sensation I wanted to focus on, the chills and the electrifying tingling swarming throughout my body. I don't remember lying back on the bed, but at one point, I was so sure that I was floating a few inches above the mattress that I reached out to check for myself.

The weird thing is that the entire tingling sensation seemed to focus on a single point, a tiny dot in the middle of my lower back. I wanted to scratch that spot, to rub my fingernails across that sensation like an annoying itch. The only reason I didn't was because I was too afraid I might scratch it out of existence. I wanted that feeling to last forever.

That night, I experienced one of the most exotic, toe-curling experiences of my life, an overwhelming rush of warmth that felt like the most comforting, most erotic hug imaginable. Whatever had invaded me did so without an ounce of effort. It was as if I subconsciously willed it myself, an essence of pure emotion turning every piece of my soul into an explosion of ecstasy. I don't know how to describe it any other way. How does one put into words an overwhelming sense of bliss that touches every tiny part of you?

I floated on air that night, the sensation lasting for what I assumed to have been hours. I don't remember falling asleep, nor Adam climbing in beside me, but at some point, we both ended up in bed together, and both of us naked. It was only when I woke up some time late the next morning that I found Adam's head lying on my stomach and a thin line of drool running from his mouth down my waist. I didn't move at first; the effort needed to keep my eyes open was already more than I could muster. I could hear conversations out in the hallway, the faint hum of traffic on the main road, as well as a plane flying somewhere in the distance.

What got me eventually moving was the cramping pressure in my bladder, the urgent need to pee eventually growing enough for me to try and pull myself out from under Adam's torso. He groaned as I rolled out from under him, and when I pushed myself off the bed. I saw him drag the blanket over himself and continue sleeping. I got dressed as best as I could and headed out into the hallway and down to the bathroom.

Once I finished peeing, and I was washing my hands, I caught my reflection in the mirror, and I could not ignore the sudden rush of shame that came over me. I couldn't stop looking at myself, the look of guilt so clearly etched on my face. It honestly felt like I was looking at the reflection of my mother and not me, her needing to show me another reminder about the pot calling the kettle black.

I felt disgusted with myself, and yet a part of me knew that there would be no escape for me, not after such an intimate experience. I wondered whether my experience had been the same as everybody else, whether that incredible tingling was the reason people became so addicted to the drug in the first place. I know people had all sorts of addictions, from sex to alcohol, to any number of drugs, but mine felt different. Perhaps it was due to my age or inexperience. What I experienced hit me on so many different levels that I couldn't imagine anybody else feeling the same.

Adam was gone by the time I got back to the room; the only sign he'd been there at all was the cigarette butts in the ashtray. I could still smell the faint hint of his body spray in the air. When I lay back down on the bed and wrapped the blanket around myself, it felt like I had travelled a thousand miles through the jungles of self-discovery. All I knew was that I had to find a way to get back to that same state of being as I had found myself the previous evening, and at that point in time, I would have given anything to do so.

CHAPTER 15

They say lightning doesn't strike the same place twice, and yet those same people tend to say that when it comes to families, lightning *always* strikes twice. Take my mother, for example. A woman whom I never knew on a personal level, and yet I found out so much about her from those who knew her the most…her family. I don't know why I would have assumed she was different from her brothers and sisters, when most of what I heard about her seemed to mirror that of an entire neighbourhood. Perhaps it was more of that arrogance I didn't know I had, the kind that assumed I was above all of that when, in truth, I was mirroring her actions almost perfectly.

The first time I tried heroin, it just about flipped my soul upside down and rearranged my brain. I couldn't think of anything else the next few weeks and months, and I found myself constantly chasing my next high any way I could. Adam once told me that he was sorry for getting me high that first time, but I didn't care, and when he refused to give me more, I simply cut him loose and found someone who would.

That little princess you began reading about at the start of this series had well and truly disappeared by this point in her story, and what you have now is a junkie chasing her next hit. The system that had always tried to make itself out to be some sort of saviour cut me free almost as easily as I did my boyfriends, who couldn't give me what I needed. Adam turned into Dave, and Dave into Rory. Rory is the one who got me pregnant a second time, and another miscarriage saved me from more potential headaches.

Would it surprise you to learn that the first time I prostituted myself for a hit was on my fifteenth birthday? I had still been seeing Rory at the time, but he had been out of town with his mother and, with me desperate for a taste, I offered to sleep with one of his friends for a price. Said friend accepted and ended up buying enough gear for us to last the entire weekend. Rory found us in bed together, smacked his mate in the head, and spat in my face. I didn't care. I barely felt it, still flying high as a kite and mostly oblivious to the argument.

There were times when I did ease off the drugs, especially when I started hanging around with a girl named Melanie March, a friend whom I met at a party I had gone to with Rory. While the relationship with him might have dissolved with that whole cheating thing, my friendship with Melanie only grew stronger. It's funny how some advice is discarded but other advice is taken on board faster than ever. Melanie suggested I let her help me get a job with this modelling agency she'd been doing part-time work for, but the prospect of a job frightened me. I wasn't sure whether I was ready for such a commitment, and if I need to be honest, working ten-hour days for the same kind of money I could make with just a single client in an hour didn't really compare.

It was around the same time that one of my aunties offered me a place to live. She had been renting this home through some government housing place, and given the size of it, she wanted someone to share it with. Maggie even promised to hold off charging me anything until I got on my feet, and it sounded too good to be true. I had always liked Maggie. She was the youngest of my aunties, and also the one closest to my mother. Maggie used to tell me that she and my mother used to think of themselves as best friends instead of sisters.

"It just sounded closer," she told me, preferring to call my mother her bestie.

I had my own room at Maggie's, and with the house having two bathrooms, I also got one of those exclusively to myself. Her boyfriend didn't come around that often since he was in the army, which meant that the house wasn't exactly a hive of activity aside from when we were both home. She worked at a hair salon during the day, and sometimes, my aunt would use me as a kind of guinea pig to practice on. I didn't mind, of course, not with free hair treatments and styles every other week.

The thing is, I started bringing clients home more and more often during those weeks. I figured that since the house was empty and I had a perfectly good bed at home, why should I waste time trying to find a hotel room? I didn't see the danger in it, a stupid move on my part, I know, but I was still young and fairly immature. Unfortunately, boobs didn't come with common sense.

The main kind of client I looked for was businessmen much older than myself, the reason being that they tended to be far more composed. Young guys just rushed me like a bull at a gate, and a few went as far as to hurt me during their brief moment of ecstasy. I wasn't exactly the strongest person, and preferring a gentle client, I tried to steer myself towards those aged at least fifty-plus. A few years under was OK if I could sense a softer disposition.

The problems began when Maggie took on a second job down at a bar and eventually met a random foreigner. She disappeared completely out of the blue one night, leaving me to run the house on my own. She once told me that the rent got paid automatically, but the utilities and groceries were a weekly thing. It wasn't long after her disappearance that I began to panic, especially when my own funds started running dry. That was when I began bringing more and more clients into my home, and it was one of those who eventually made me see the error of my ways.

I cannot tell you his name because I had stopped caring about their individual identities. No…no, that's not true. It wasn't because I no longer cared about who they were. The reality was that I didn't want to remember them that way. Looking at oneself in the mirror gets tougher each time you sell a little more of yourself, and I had done a lot of selling in those days. It felt like I had sold off almost half of my soul and each time I saw myself in the mirror, the face staring back at me felt more like a stranger.

The client who ended up as my final one ever shouldn't have been in my house at all. He shouldn't have been a client to begin with because of a promise I had once made with myself. I almost made myself promise that if my gut told me not to go with some-one, then I would trust my instincts, regardless of how desperate I was at the time. I should have listened to my inner self and saved myself the pain.

I had been hanging around a local train station that morning because I had walked one of my friends there. She was scared to go alone as her boyfriend had made some pretty significant threats against her, and, not wanting to walk alone, I had gone with her. I wanted to wait until her train had gone, and it was while waving to her that a man approached me asking if I knew where the closest ATM was.

He was smartly dressed, just like I preferred, and I guessed his age to have been somewhere north of forty-five. The man wore a moustache, and his smile showed a perfect row of white teeth. When he first approached me, I could smell the expensive cologne, and I immediately saw through his facade when something inside me tightened.

"There's one two blocks down," I told him, pointing to the right side of the main road.

"OK, good," he said, his grin never leaving his face. He looked me up and down, spending an extra second on my bust. "And how much do I need to take out if I want to spend a couple of hours with you?" He asked, lowering his tone to keep the question between us.

My first instinct was to yell at him, to tell him to beat it and not insult me like that. Did I really make it that obvious? I wasn't sure and didn't think I advertised my services quite so openly. And besides, it wasn't as if I was doing it full-time. I still considered the act as nothing more than desperation, even if I had been offered alternatives along the way. But then again, a job is a job, and I really didn't want to pass up the chance to make a bit of extra money.

"Two hundred," I told him, raising my usual number on account of him looking like he could afford it. Maybe that had been my mistake. In any case, I could have told him a thousand times, and it wouldn't have made a difference to the end result.

"Sounds reasonable," he told me and beckoned for me to follow. "I'm George," he told me as we walked, and something about his tone told me it wasn't. That was fine by me, since clients had a tendency to lie about their real identity. I did the same. It wasn't as if my real name was Candy, or Cherry, or whatever name I happened to feel like sharing at the time.

We walked to the ATM, where George took out an amount of money. I can't tell you how much because I didn't see it properly. He pulled it from the dispensing slot and slipped it into his pocket before he turned back towards me, and we simply continued on to my house. George was a bit of a talker and shared details about his job as a banker and how he had never been married and hoped to one day find a suitable lady.

I knew bullshit when I heard it, and even at fifteen, I could see through his. The man wanted one thing, and I think talking was how he kept his nerves in check. He seemed surprised when we reached my house, but didn't complain, especially when I walked him to the bedroom and told him to get comfortable. I went to the bathroom and prepared myself.

When the act itself finished some twenty minutes later, George's mood changed immediately. He began to tell me that I hadn't earned my money and so didn't deserve any of it. He kept going on about him needing to do all the work, despite him insisting on getting on top. When I tried to grab some of the cash from his pants pocket, he slapped me hard enough across the face to send me sprawling to the ground. That in itself wasn't enough for him, and after getting dressed, he walked to where I was still lying, leaned down, grabbed a handful of my hair and punched me in the face.

What followed were two brutal minutes of a man beating a helpless girl senseless. It was as if the sex had only been the encore for him, the beating the main event. Each time I saw his face, that same grin stared back at me, those perfect white teeth almost mocking me. He slapped my face multiple times, the sound echoing through the room like gunshots. Not content with just my face, he also kicked me each time I fell to the ground, his expensive leather shoes feeling like steel-capped boots.

I don't remember passing out or him leaving. All I remember is coming to some time later and hearing Jack's voice somewhere in the distance. I do remember calling out to him, but I think I lost consciousness again before he got to me. The next thing I knew was me lying in bed with my ribcage feeling on fire and Jack leaning over me with a cold dishcloth pressed to my face. He looked white as a ghost, with the fear somehow mirrored between us. He kept going on about needing to call an ambulance, but the last thing I wanted was to answer questions about a stranger being in my bedroom.

Jack saved my life, of that I have little doubt. If he hadn't found me when he did, I might have died right here on the floor. But that's not the only reason. I never told Jack this, but I swear that some time during the night, I saw a face staring in at us through the bedroom window, a face that I immediately recognised. It was the same man who had caused the injuries in the first place, and I have no doubt in my mind that he had come back to finish the job. Perhaps he was scared that I would report him to the police, that I would press charges and disrupt his life. Or, perhaps he was some kind of serial killer and beating me was just the beginning of how he liked to torture his victims.

In any case, that night, I made a pact with myself, one that I believed I would hang onto for the rest of my life. I knew I had been taking risks, risks that I could have avoided if I had been more focused on my well-being. The unfortunate thing is that sometimes, circumstances require more desperate measures, and it is that very thinking that I would come to fall for again and again. Despite the risks, there were moments in my life where desperate measures proved too strong and I would repeatedly fall into the grips of despair.

CHAPTER 16

Sometimes I wonder about the sorts of friends I should have made during those dark years of my life, back when it felt like I had finally taken some sort of control over my life. I did return to Blackrock House a number of times due to a shortage in other places like St. Agnes. Speaking of St. Agnes, I did go back at one point, just to pay a visit and catch up with the likes of Sister Alice and Sister Hope. Unfortunately, those visits also proved to be a mistake, not because of anything that was said, but rather because of what was not said.

The more you fend for yourself on the streets, the more in tune you become with the people around you. I find that as the years passed by, I could read people far more easily, with their eyes often offering the clearest insight into the person behind the face. While some people might try to hide their feelings with fake compliments and even faker smiles, nothing could hide the contempt in their eyes.

I have to admit, I mightn't have been in the best of shape when I went to St. Agnes to say hi. I know of lots of girls who would do the same while I lived there, and each time the sisters would welcome them with open arms and sit down for long talks about times gone by. Not so with me. Not only did I sense a certain uncomfortableness from both sisters, but Sister Alice proved to be the most surprising one of all when she hesitated to hug me. I saw the shock in her eyes when she saw me, and it was something I found myself unable to get past.

I cried when I walked out of the home that final time, although I made sure not to let anybody see me. I hung onto my emotions until I was well down the street, and only then, a few tears escaped. How can I describe the feeling of finding out that the one place where I felt at home suddenly turned into nothing more than a confused memory? I didn't blame the sisters, of course. Why would I? I had lost a lot of weight because of my drug use, and had pierced my nose. I had also let Melanie shave almost half my head, which only added to the complete mirror image of the girl I used to be. Or, perhaps it was the tracks on my arms they saw.

In any case, I messed up by making a last-minute decision to visit, and I paid the price. I fixed my mood with a hit later that afternoon and ended up sleeping through the night, while some guy I had been seeing used my body for his own entertainment. He was also the one who bought the drugs, so we both kind of won.

Unfortunately, things took another turn a couple of days later when Melanie came rushing into my room and shouted about the two of us taking a trip. I hadn't quite woken up, so it took me a few minutes to understand what she was saying, but once she slowed down and sat next to me, my brain finally caught up.

"I got you a job," she told me. "My boss has been screaming for someone to help out during the Paris Fashion Show next week and I suggested you."

"Fashion?" I couldn't make sense of what she meant since I had neither experience nor interest in fashion. I pictured having to get dressed in skimpy clothes and walk up and down some runway while people ogled at me and took photographs. As it turned out, the role wasn't quite that fashionable.

"No, silly," Melanie said. "She needs a runner to work in the back dressing rooms. It's what *I* do. We have to run pieces of clothing between all of the dressing stations and the central hub. It gets really busy and there's like a thousand people back there."

"Do they pay?" It was the first question that came to mind, no surprise considering how broke I was.

"Of course, she pays you. As long as you do the work right. Oh, and she's Katherine with a k, just to be sure."

"I can do the work," I said, and just about fell out of bed when Melanie leaned over to hug me.

The real excitement didn't really hit me until after I met with Jack and told him of my plans. I don't know why, but I think it had to do with my needing to share the news with someone who mattered. Melanie was my friend, of course, but our friendship didn't compare to the one I had with Jack. I did go and see Ollie first, though, but given that he was sitting inside a prison cell in nearby Feltham, it didn't make things easy. I found it impossibly difficult to remain positive, seeing him like that, and while he was happy for me, I could tell another little piece of him had died. When I eventually met with Jack, I kept to myself what I saw with Ollie. I didn't want to worry him any more than I had to.

That's the problem with having friends who are so close. We each carried around so many issues of our own that it made it hard to talk about someone else's issues. I doubt Jack needed to hear about Ollie doing it tough in that jail, just as I found it impossibly hard seeing him like that. All I could think of was my guilt of wanting to turn around and walk out as soon as I could.

I guess, in a way, those two meetings were the goodbye I needed before leaving. It wasn't a permanent goodbye, of course, but one that still needed to be said. With their blessing, I now felt ready to go and explore a new side of the world I had only ever dreamed about, a world that I wasn't entirely sure wanted me to be a part of it.

Melanie and I first headed to central London, where a bus

carrying several models and technical staff was waiting for us. My friend introduced me to as many people as she could, but it was the models I found myself immediately drawn to. Casey really stood out to me, not only because she came across as the friendliest, but because I found out through Melanie that she had spent a brief moment of her childhood at a similar home to St. Agnes. Unlike me, however, she had been adopted by a family when she was just seven years old and had been sent to some of the finest schools in the country.

The bus took us all to the train station, and we arrived in Paris several hours later. While we had travelled mostly as a group, we quickly dispersed the moment we reached the hotel. It turned out that we weren't all booked into the same place. Not only did Melanie and I share a room with two other girls employed as runners, but our hotel was situated about three blocks from the Ritz, the place where the models, the boss and her closest support crew were staying.

"You girls are located much closer to the convention centre, so I expect you to be there early," Katherine, with a k, told us when she directed us to the hotel. I still wasn't sure how to take my new boss. She always spoke with an air of sophistication whenever important people were around, but then I'd hear her talk to one of the staff, and this old town drawl would fall from her lips.

"She's nice, trust me," Melanie told me more than a few times, and I wasn't sure whether she was trying to convince me or herself.

The thing is, Melanie had definitely been right about one thing. The job was amazing. Not only that, but it opened doors for us that I could only have ever dreamed about before landing this job. While the pay wasn't too bad for someone my age, it was the extra benefits that proved to be the real bonus. I'm talking about the connections, the parties, the random trips while at shows. That first event proved to be a stepping stone for us, which ultimately led to many more.

The problems didn't really arise for a number of years. They rarely do when you're flying high on life itself, and with the shows running for most of the year, our lives cycled from one event to the next, made up of work during the day and parties at night. We often hung out with the models, namely because they had the connections to get us into the truly exotic places and for us, that meant access to places far out of our reach. And how the drugs and drink kept flowing.

By 2004, Melanie and I had reached a point in our lives where we took a bold step into adulthood for real with our eighteenth birthdays just days apart. The parties were nothing short of mind-blowing, with Casey often right behind us. She made far more money than we did and always knew where to go when it came time to liven things up. She had friends in all levels of the business, and given her incredible beauty, she also had men practically falling on their knees for her. Given her insatiable appetite for attention, she also used it to her advantage as much as possible.

The problem with Casey was that she didn't know her limits, not with drugs, not with alcohol, and certainly not with sex. She struggled with all of her vices, although she always avoided talking about them directly, especially with us. Melanie and I were usually there to pick up the pieces when things really took a turn, but Casey would just shrug them aside, wait until the next party and then get back on the proverbial horse.

Things really came to a head in the summer of 2005. Melanie had already been promoted to design assistant, and Katherine had told me that I would be taking up a position within her direct team the following month when one of her assistants was taking off for maternity leave. It felt like promotions were raining down all around us, and life was about to get even better than any of us could have imagined. We had also been back in London for the week, which Casey saw as another opportunity to party things up while back in our home town.

With everybody having something to celebrate, it wasn't really a question of who would go. The previous couple of weeks had been tough on all of us, with three shows in two cities and numerous events in between. Katherine virtually ran the legs off us, and Casey wanted us to enjoy our downtime. She had organised a big night on the town for us, with dinner, drinks, and a huge party afterwards, hosted by one of her friends who had just gotten engaged. Maybe it was because of that engagement announcement that things got so out of hand.

I didn't know it at the time, but I learned later that Casey had been having issues with her own insecurities. It wasn't often that she brought up her past, but when she did, it was usually because of flashbacks to her time in the system, back when she struggled to find any sort of self-identity. Modelling saved her, in a way, but only as far as showing her that possibilities weren't out of reach for some rag brigade drop-out, as she called herself.

The guy who her friend got engaged to also happened to be the same guy Casey lost her virginity to, a guy that had been within her circle for years. She never got over losing him and had been secretly plotting to try to win him back. The engagement effectively ended that dream, and Casey was left licking her invisible wounds.

We arrived at the party a little after ten that night, and right before going in, Casey handed me a small pack of pills, not unusual for her to do. Given how she lacked the discipline to limit herself, she preferred someone else to hold her supply in case she went overboard. What I didn't know at the time was that she had already popped a few and would be taking other drugs once inside. It wasn't as if I was her carer and would be keeping her on a leash.

I could see her pain almost immediately. The hugs with both her friend and the woman's fiancé, the wince when Vicky showed off the ring, and the fake excitement when she heard the date for the wedding. Casey did well to put on a brave face, but it was never going to last. She hit the bar the first chance she got, latched on to the nearest guy, and practically ran for the dance floor, ending up close to the speakers so as to drown out her inner demons.

When the overdose eventually hit, I wasn't in the yard at all, but in the bathroom trying to wash a wine stain from my top thanks to an overzealous dancing partner. The commotion spread like wildfire, with people panicking and shouting for an ambulance. It was

Melanie who found her first and subsequently called me over. I remember standing there watching this fiancé and another guy desperately performing CPR on her, but I somehow knew she was gone long before the paramedics ever showed up. The way her glazed-over eyes stared out into the void with no substance behind them, no soul left to peer into the world. She was just…gone.

The next few hours became a mass of confusion as the police eventually arrived, and after they spent time taking witness statements, I somehow ended up in a police interview room with the contents of my purse spread across the table, including the pills Casey had given me to mind for her. Imagine trying to talk yourself out of that dilemma. A friend has just overdosed on the very same pills you have in abundance in a bag that you carried around at the party.

What I should have known at the time was that alliances are only ever as strong as the people behind them. No, maybe alliances is the wrong word here. Friendships. Friendships are only ever as strong as the people behind them. Unfortunately for me, I had been blinded by the glitz and glamour of our lives, the endless parties and attention we were getting just by working our jobs. What I didn't know was that one of my closest friends was about to betray me in the worst way possible.

What I didn't know at the time was that Casey had also handed Melanie a bag of pills, the same ones she had handed me. I guess she wanted to ensure easy access to them whenever she wanted a couple, and so had both of us carry them around. Melanie had been the one to give Casey the extra pills. When Casey overdosed, Melanie dumped her bag into the toilet before the police arrived and, during the interviews, told them about the bag I was holding to turn their attention away from her. She lied to save her own arse and, in the process, threw me under the bus in the worst way possible.

After seven hours of sitting through relentless questioning, I was formally charged with manslaughter, as well as multiple other charges relating to the possession and distribution of the pills. I could barely speak; the shock of what had happened was too much for me to comprehend. One of my best friends had died, another had betrayed me, and I now faced the serious prospect of prison. It felt like my life had taken a sharp turn south and wasn't going to get better any time soon.

CHAPTER 17

Nothing brings reality to the forefront like finding yourself in a police holding cell. I know, because I had been there a couple of times before that night, both times for possession. The officers who had brought me in during those times when I was sixteen and seventeen had promised not to bring up the fact that I had been prostituting myself, and only charged me for the small amount of heroin they found on me. A significant break, you might think, but not when you've been brought in a third time, facing manslaughter charges for allegedly supplying the victim with drugs.

Oh, the irony. An arrest and subsequent court appearance that had once felt like a reprieve now came back to haunt me as I faced a third-strike situation, and not one that I could talk my way out of. I'm not sure why Katherine with a K paid for one, but I ended up with a barrister named Kelly Mann, and she warned right from the very beginning that I would be looking at jail time.

"Given the circumstances surrounding your previous charges, I'd say you're going to be in for quite a fight," she told me during that first interview.

"But I'm innocent," I said, words I was sure she had heard a million times before and normally uttered by people with their crimes still fresh on their breath.

"Guilty or innocent isn't the issue here," Kelly said. "Given your previous record, the judge is going to take one look and see a pattern. You can understand that, right?"

"I do understand that," I said. "But I'm still innocent. Casey gave me those pills to hold for her. I've never used them. Check me. Take a blood sample." I spat the words out like bullets, wishing each one to hit its mark and save me from prison, but I knew the chances of that happening were slim to none.

The best we can hope for in the immediate future is for me to apply for bail so that you can at least spend the next few weeks out of jail. What happens after that is anyone's guess."

Hope is a funny thing when facing such a tragic case of mistaken identity. You can long for it as much as you want, but somewhere in the back of your mind, you already know the end result long before it actually happens. I knew I was going to end up in jail that day, and not her promises or guidance were going to change that. In a way, the decision had already been made long before Casey had even died, thanks to my own stupidity. And it was because of that stupidity that the process felt like it was on rails, with me strapped into a seat and unable to fight my way out of it.

True to her word, Kelly did manage to get me bail, but not until I spent another couple of days in lock-up. Let me tell you, there isn't a lot of dignity left when you're forced to pee in front of thirty other women in a place where privacy is almost non-existent. I wasn't always in the communal holding cell. I think it came down to a matter of supply and demand, as I eventually found myself moved into a much smaller cell with three others. It still meant taking care of your bathroom needs in front of a crowd, but at least the crowd was considerably smaller.

I think one of the most common questions I was asked by other girls had to do with the reason I had been locked up in the first place. Drugs seemed to be the most common reason, with prostitution second. There was a habitual drunk driver in the cell with us, as well as another woman for assault. I was the only one facing manslaughter, and it became apparent that I had my work cut out for me, so to speak. The expressions on girls' faces when I told them why I was there were enough for me to feel the pressure; an uncomfortable smile was my only reply to their usual comment of, "Damn, good luck with that."

By the time I reached the courtroom, I had virtually lost all hope of getting out of the place. Other than to visit Ollie, I had never been inside a proper jail, with the holding cells at the police station scary enough for me. The prospect of me moving up in the world felt a thousand times worse, and I could barely breathe, let alone walk into the courtroom to find out my immediate fate.

I don't know how she managed to do it, but I ended up getting bail on the condition that I remain at a fixed address, which Kelly put down as Katherine's. One of my former boss's assistants had been present in the court and acted on her behalf, although I never spoke with her directly. As it turned out, they didn't really care about the specifics, with Kelly asking if I had a safe place to stay until my case went to trial.

"Yes, I do," I told her, although she never asked where. I think it had to do with money, since Katherine had plenty of it and knew how to manipulate the system.

Somehow, I ended up with Jack at his place and spent almost an entire month with him. No, there was nothing intimate about the arrangement, if you were wondering. The entire stay was purely platonic, if you can believe that. I don't think either one of us wanted to risk the friendship, which I had seen happen to others who crossed the line into some sort of relationship. To me, a friendship with someone I had known and trusted for so long was far more valuable to me than the chance of intimacy. I wasn't about to risk what we had for a few minutes of passion. Ollie would also come over, but he didn't hang around for long, despite my needing support. I think he still had too many of his own demons to deal with, and seeing me only seemed to amplify his own.

The month flew by much faster than I had hoped. In the beginning, it felt like I had an infinite amount of time between me and what fate had in store, but as the days began to pass by, it honestly felt like time had somehow sped up. The week before the scheduled court appearance just about flew by in the blink of an eye. I did meet with Kelly a couple of times during that final week, with her still trying to open my mind up to the two options before us.

I struggled on so many levels during that month, I can't even begin to tell you how much. One friend was dead, another had betrayed me, and I faced a wall of charges that had the potential to send me away for years. It's tough trying to figure out where it all went wrong, and I often wondered whether my inaction played a deciding role in Casey's death. Maybe instead of using her popularity for my own gratification, I should have been the voice of reason and perhaps tried to help Casey with her addiction.

Who am I kidding? We were all guilty of things, Casey, Melanie, me, all of us in the same boat, happy to pop pills like gumdrops and guzzle booze like fizzy drinks. None of us had any interest in thinking about words like reality, consequences, and repercussions. We did what we did because we liked it and I joined in as much as any of them. The question Kelly kept wanting me to ask myself, however, was whether I was guilty or not.

Did I have a guilty conscience about Casey's death? Hell yes, who wouldn't? I've asked myself the same questions a thousand times over and each time I come up with a different answer than the last. Was I actually guilty of manslaughter, though? Absolutely not. I did a favour for a friend because she asked it of me, but at no time did I ply her full of pills that I bought for the purpose of distribution. I didn't give her those pills any more than I didn't give her the alcohol that boosted the effects of the drugs and subsequently sent her overboard.

The real dilemma came from the reasons behind the decision I had to make. If there's one thing about Kelly I appreciated, it was that she didn't mince her words. She said things the way they were, without trying to sugarcoat it.

"If you continue pleading not guilty and forcing the court to sit through a trial and you're found guilty, the judge *will* hand down the maximum sentence," was what she told me, and not just once. "Emma, you could face spending the next twenty years behind bars. Plead guilty, on the other hand, and you could be out in as soon as six months, maybe less, if the judge is feeling generous and you catch him in a good mood."

The decision I had to face wasn't about right or wrong, but about whether I valued my time. I remember one particular conversation Jack and I had during those final few days and how I shouldn't worry about what others might think of me.

"Who cares what anybody else thinks," he said, shaking his head in frustration. "Nothing is going to bring your friend back and as far as the judge is concerned, you have a history of drug possession, so there's that."

He had a point, of course. Screw morals or ethics or whatever else you want to call it. This wasn't about whether I had played a part in Casey's death. This was whether I wanted to spend months inside, or years. I had to decide whether I would take responsibility for her death and cop the punishment, or fight for the truth and risk my entire future. Six months versus twenty years. What would you have done? I know there will be those who would never admit to something they weren't guilty of, regardless of the ramifications. Some people will stick to their guns no matter what, and when I began that month, that's exactly how I felt.

When I walked into that courtroom, I swear you could have heard a pin drop, and I'm surprised I didn't bring up my breakfast that I didn't want to eat, but did because Jack had insisted. My nerves were shot, but worse than that, I started suffering severe depression the previous couple of days and not even Jack's support helped me. I felt like the world was about to end for me and all I wanted to do was run.

The other thing is, I still maintained my commitment to the Not Guilty plea. It felt wrong not to, since I hadn't done anything wrong. I remember every set of eyes turning to watch me walk in, especially Casey's family, who looked at me with so much hatred. I wanted to die right there and then, and would have gladly jumped into a hole if one had opened up in front of me.

I don't know why, but something about the moment when the judge walked into the courtroom rattled me. It could have been the overwhelming silence hanging in the air, the serious look of utter contempt on the judge's face, or me hearing the beating in my chest, but something made me change my mind at the last minute. I leaned over to Kelly and, without thinking, I whispered the words I had been dreading for an entire month. I'm not sure whether she just didn't hear me or couldn't believe I said them at all, but my barrister looked at me with complete surprise on her face. I nodded, reaffirming what I had just said. I expected her to maybe ask for a recess so she could speak to me more directly, but, surprising me yet again, Kelly turned to the bench and ended my speculation.

"Your Honour, if I may," Kelly said, projecting her voice across the courtroom.

"What is it, Ms Mann?" The judge looked down at us over the rim of his gold-wired glasses with that same frumpy tone I remembered from my first appearance.

"Your Honour, if it pleases the court, my client wishes to change her plea to guilty."

A subdued murmur rolled across the courtroom the second the words left my barrister's lips, and one look from the judge silenced them again.

"Does your client understand what it will mean in terms of her trial?"

"She does, Your Honour."

The system barely flinched as the judge turned the trial into a sentencing session. I had barely time to blink before I had to stand and confirm my plea. The judge nodded appreciatively, kept me standing and announced that he would sentence me without delay. I looked at my barrister with disbelief, as I didn't think it would happen quite so fast.

When the judge read the sentence out loud, I remember screaming in disbelief as someone behind me cheered. All the strength ran out of my legs, and I tried to sit back down on the chair, but it slid out from under me, and I ended up on the floor. I barely heard the four-year sentence, my heart sinking when he announced a non-parole period of two. Two whole years, a far cry from the six months I had been led to believe I would get. Jack told me later that Kelly tried to apologise to me repeatedly, but I don't remember that at all. It's hard to hear words when dragged out of a room by a bunch of officers.

Three days before my nineteenth birthday, I left the courtroom in handcuffs with a custodial sentence hanging over my head. What I remember most about the subsequent ride to the jail aboard a prison bus is the feeling of utter helplessness. It wasn't until that moment that I truly understood what freedom really meant. That was the moment I completely lost mine.

CHAPTER 18

The second I stepped off that prison bus, the reality set in for me. I've heard some people say that it happens when you end up in a cell and the door slams shut, while others say they felt it the moment the cuffs closed around their wrists. Everyone is different, I guess, but for me, it happened when the door to my compartment opened and a prison officer called for us to exit the bus and stand on the line. The three of us climbed down the single step and into a yard surrounded by high walls and razor wire.

The intimidation of the place hit me from the get-go, with the officers speaking to us as if we were soldiers or something. They'd bark orders, and if we didn't react quickly enough, they'd close in and start yelling. A couple of the girls didn't take too kindly to being bossed around and tried to yell back, but these officers merely shrugged it off like it was nothing. I could tell they were used to it, and while those women tried their hardest to insult them, the abuse fell rather flat.

I felt like a zombie that first day, moving through each step in the process as if I was again strapped to some rollercoaster seat and sent down the track. Orders came from everywhere, and I found myself going through medical examinations, strip searches, and interviews, with the questions feeling nothing more than rehearsed protocol. Those asking the questions didn't show a shred of interest in my answers and normally just sat stone-faced while typing those answers into their computers.

There must have been about two dozen women going through the same process as me. Every now and then, we'd end up in this communal holding cell after finishing each part of the admission. Someone brought us food at one point, and I think it was the first time since arriving that everybody shut up. The food tasted alright, I guess, but lacked any kind of love, if that makes sense. The stew tasted plastic, worse than airline food, and lacked any sort of recognisable flavour, not that I cared.

The only person who showed any interest in me was a woman named Shona. I think she must have been aged somewhere in her early forties, although she never came right out and said so, not even after asking me how old I was. She told me that I reminded her of her daughter, which was why she was talking with me. Apparently, she had a similar hair colour to mine and might have been the same age. I'm not really too sure, to be honest, as my attention span wasn't huge, given the nerves still wreaking havoc on me.

One of the things that really stood out to me during those first few hours was the noise, a kind of relentless background track of yelling, banging, and non-stop chattering. Someone was always holding a conversation, either nearby or further afield, and there seemed to be constant doors opened and closed, each time accompanied by keys rattling in locks. I flinched hard each time someone yelled or cried out or kicked a door, the echoes loud enough to hurt my ears.

Shona tried her best to calm me during those first few hours. She told me about how she had served time for battery ten years earlier, an incident she claimed she didn't regret at all since it had been against her ex-husband. She said the man was a pig and had cheated on Shona with her best friend, a woman she had known since high school. I tried to listen as much as possible, but with so many distractions surrounding us, it became almost impossible.

I thought the most challenging part of that afternoon was arriving at the prison and not knowing what would happen, but all of that paled in comparison to when they escorted me and three others to a nearby unit. We had to walk down these narrow walkways and corridors, and each time we stepped out of a building, the chorus of voices calling out to us sounded like a grandstand of crazed soccer fans. A couple of the girls simply laughed it off and waved, even going as far as calling out to some of those mockers by name. I quickly learned that they were considered regulars inside the place, with one only absent for about a month before being thrown back inside.

The moment I walked into the unit, I knew I had messed up big time. Tragic doesn't even begin to explain how I saw the situation. It felt like a hundred people stared at me as I walked through that door, with half of them whispering something to the other half. I could hear giggles, people calling to others about the newbies arriving. I saw a couple of heads pop out of their respective cells to look for themselves and then murmur something to others standing nearby.

A few girls didn't stop at just looking or whispering. They called out actual insults, maybe needing to prove their authority within the unit. I understood there was a pecking order of sorts, but to be honest, the only thing I cared about at that moment was making it through the next two years.

Two years. I could hardly believe it, and when I eventually made it to my new cell, I whispered the number to myself while staring at the pathetic sheet of foam serving as my mattress. It looked like dogs had used it, the dirty smears streaking the fabric from one side to the other. I had a bedsheet amongst the bundle of things handed to me at the dispensing window, but just seeing it like that solidified my situation.

"Unit is currently locked down," the officer told us as she

walked us into the place. She dropped each of us into our cells in turn, finishing with me up on the second floor.

The cell was about as plain as you could imagine. A single bunk bed, with the top already occupied. A stainless steel toilet bowl stood behind a waist-high divider that didn't leave a lot to the imagination, with a sink attached to the wall next to it. A kind of desk and shelf were fixed to the far end of the wall, and next to that, a narrow window covered in steel bars. Together, those individual bits made up the majority of my new existence, a depressive combination of frugal convenience.

"You the new girl?"

I looked up to see the side of a foot dangling over the edge of the top bunk, an incessant shaking reminding me of impatience. The woman who lay there sounded more male than Jack or Ollie, and I felt my insides tighten a bit further.

"Yes," I said, trying to sound as cheerful as possible, or maybe it was confidence I was hoping for. "I'm Emma," I added, hoping that I didn't sound completely overwhelmed.

"If you need a shit, do it in the communal toilets at the end of the corridor," was the response I got, a far cry from the introduction I had expected.

Leona Lewis wasn't the kind of woman who suffered idiots, or so she told me when she eventually rolled off the side of the bed and jumped to the floor. She stood just a fraction shorter than me, but had the physique of a body builder. Aside from the noticeable bustline, she could have passed for a man, given how defined her muscle tone was. She had more muscles than any woman I had ever seen, and the attitude to go with them.

"First time?" I nodded, unsure of what else to offer. Leona wasn't looking for more and squatted on the toilet as I dropped my belongings onto the lower bed.

I tried to block out the sounds of her using the facilities as much as possible, but how do you block out that metallic twang of forced urine hitting metal in an enclosed space? I felt the heat of embarrassment rising in my cheeks, but that paled in comparison to when the smell of that piss actually hit, a scent I couldn't escape from. I almost breathed a sigh of relief when I heard the toilet flush, although I didn't make it obvious as I continued setting up my bed.

"You'll want to store your things up on that shelf," Leona said when she finished washing her hands. "I got mine on the shelf above my bed."

"How long have you been here?" I asked, hoping to generate some form of conversation to help me settle down a bit, but the response I got told me everything I needed to know.

"Too long," Leona said, and before I could ask anything else, she had climbed back up onto the top bunk and rolled over to face the wall, leaving me looking at her back.

I unpacked my bag and then pushed it under the bed for safe-keeping. The rest of my things took up about half the shelf, made up of nothing but toiletries and clothing. Unsure of what I could bring, I left most of my things back at Jack's, not that I had much. When you grow up in the system like me, material possessions generally don't exist, not unless you either stole them or had them given to you, and there is a very good reason for it.

I believe that most people are nothing more than a product of their environment. They tend to believe in the same things as those around them, and will often adopt mannerisms and characteristics similar to friends and family members. Their wealth is also usually proportional to their background, with most families sharing similar financial standings. Those of us who are part of the rag brigade aren't that much different.

Take me, for example. Anything I brought with me to St. Agnes way back in those early years ended up either stolen or worn out within a very short space of time. The people who asked to play with my toys didn't care for them the way I did, and so handled those things without care. Why would a kid respect my things when the majority of them never had anything for themselves?

Prison, in a generalised kind of way, felt precisely the same way that St. Agnes did in the very beginning. Filled with all manner of strangers, from bullies to thieves, from strong to weak, from introverts to extroverts. There were people brimming with confidence and others scared of their own shadows, and I had to navigate my way through the crowd to find my own place. I had returned to a place more than a little familiar without ever having set foot inside.

It wasn't long before my cellmate began snoring, a thick volume of nasal congestion filling the air. Unable to escape, I lay on my own bed and climbed under the blanket. Eventually, I pulled it far enough to cover me completely, and when that wasn't enough, I pulled the pillow over my face to shield me from those sounds. It didn't work anywhere near as well as it did when I used the method years earlier, but with little choice to do anything else, it was all I had.

We must have stayed like that for about two hours before I heard voices from out in the main common area, combined with intermittent clanking. I couldn't quite make out what they were saying, but I knew it must have had something to do with food because a new smell had begun creeping into the cell. Leona continued snoring right up until a narrow slit in the door suddenly opened and a voice called out to us.

"Grab your food," the voice called, and I got up just as Leona's feet slid around and almost hit me in the face.

"When are we being let out?" my cellmate called out as she grabbed her tray of food, the tone more demanding than inquisitive.

"Not until tomorrow," came the reply, to which Leona mumbled something else under her breath.

We each sat on our beds while eating, and while the food might have been a bit better than what I had at the holding cells, we're only talking marginally. I guess you could have called it lasagna, although the pasta sheets had been well overcooked, and the meat lacked that distinct tomato flavour. A big bruise ruined the apple, while the bread felt stale. I ate most of the lasagna and saved the apple for later, but offered the bread to my cellmate, who took it without so much as a grunt of thanks. I didn't care. I had more pressing issues to worry about.

That night turned into one of the longest of my life as I lay awake in a perpetual state of torture. I can't say it was the silence that got to me because there was none. The girls, or women rather, began to come alive around nine o'clock and didn't settle down again until around four the following morning. It sounded like an endless party, with singing and shouting and conversations that seemed to travel between cells sitting on opposite ends of the block.

I didn't want to listen to any of it, but with me unable to get away from it, I eventually began to come out of my hiding spot, pulling the blanket down so I could listen to those with whom I now shared a home. In a way, it didn't feel all that dissimilar from St. Agnes, or even Blackrock, to a certain extent. People used to hold conversations across multiple rooms there as well, although a supervisor or sister would usually interrupt at some point to bring the volume back down again. Not so in prison.

The officers didn't seem to care. Either that, or they were far enough away from the block where they didn't hear what was going on. The yelling and screaming carried on for hours, and throughout it all, my cellmate continued snoring. She did get up at one point to relieve herself, but thankfully, some of the noise from out in the unit masked her bodily sounds enough for me almost to believe they weren't happening.

I'm not sure at which point I eventually fell asleep, but I do remember using the pillow as a shield, holding it close to my chest as if hugging a dear friend and crying myself into utter exhaustion. Somewhere during those early morning hours, my body and brain just gave up fighting the urge, and I drifted off into something akin to sleep. I don't think I dreamed at all, and if I did, then it couldn't have been worthy of remembering.

CHAPTER 19

"Bottom bunk, show me movement," a voice called out, and when I finally stirred, I heard the trap in the door slam back into place.

"You'll want to answer them the first time," Leona said from somewhere closer than the top bunk, and when I turned around, I found her standing next to my bed, looking down on me. In one hand, she held her toothbrush; in the other, the paste.

"They're not known for patience," she said while squeezing some of the white paste onto the bristles. "Don't want to end up facing the turtles on your first day here."

"Turtles?" I half sat, leaning on my elbow.

"They're the ones they bring in for difficult prisoners," she said before turning away to brush her teeth.

I hadn't expected a conversation, so I wasn't prepared with questions, but, given her mood to talk, I didn't want to pass up the opportunity.

"It's hard not knowing what to do," I said, swinging my legs around and putting my feet on the floor. I rubbed my eyes and stretched when Leona didn't answer immediately.

"You'll catch on," she eventually said before rinsing her mouth.

While I didn't know what the routine would be, there was one thing I was absolutely sure about, and that was that my bladder wasn't going to hold out much longer. The pressure down there already felt more than uncomfortable, and the last thing I wanted was to wet my bed on the first morning, not when first impressions mattered so much.

With no choice but to wait, I resigned myself to the fact that I had to go at some point, and I only had one other person in the cell with me. Who knew what the communal toilets looked like? That familiar heat began to rise in my cheeks again as I sat down and let the pressure flow out of me. Leona had been humming something as she climbed back onto her bed and continued as I peed. Once done, I washed my hands and then took care of my teeth, although I really wanted a shower.

"Showers are down in the communal bathroom as well," she said as if reading my mind. "It's a good idea to wait until after lunch as they tend to fill up during the morning."

"Thanks," I said. "How hot is the water?" I wasn't sure why I asked, considering any shower was better than none at all, but I wanted to try and build some sort of rapport with a woman I would be sharing considerable time with. Or at least, that's what I thought.

The trap in the door suddenly opened, and a face appeared. I could make out the gold buttons on the officer's uniform, but not the rank emblem.

"Twenty minutes, Lewis," the officer said. "Make sure you're ready."

"Oh, I'll be ready, Miss," my cellmate said and jumped from the bunk.

It wasn't until she pulled her empty bag out from under her mattress and began throwing things into it that I realised she was leaving.

"Here, you'll want to use this," she said as she held out a brand-new cake of soap. I was about to say thank you, but then she held out a second item. "Consider it payment for handing this to Maddie."

"Maddie?"

"Cell 2S, third from the end. I'm sure she'll come and find you when the unit is unlocked again."

"What is it?" I asked as I took the single sock and felt something soft and pliable inside.

"Not something you want to be caught with," Leona said, and for the first time lowered her voice.

I considered handing both the sock and the soap back to her, but I knew that having enemies in such a place wasn't advisable, especially with my exit blocked for quite some time. I also wasn't new to the kind of people housed in the place, since the majority of them came from the very same place I grew up. It's much easier to make enemies than friends, and I preferred the latter.

"I'll do it," I said, hiding the sigh building inside me. I had barely time to tuck it under my mattress before a key invaded the door lock, and it suddenly swung open to reveal two female officers standing there.

"Alright, Lewis, time to go," one of them said while the other took a couple of steps back, eyeing me suspiciously.

I could barely move, positive that the second officer would see right through me and call for a team to flip the cell. I hated the fact that my cheeks glowed whenever I got nervous, but it was a trait I couldn't escape from, and at that moment, it felt like it was about to betray me again. The officer maintained eye contact with me for the duration of the door being open. Leona grabbed her bag and wished me luck without looking at me directly. She left the cell, and once the door was locked again, I could hear her calling out to several different people during her short walk from the unit.

The thing I found out almost immediately is that prison time is very different to any kind of time I had been exposed to. When alone in a cell and dreading every moment, each minute feels like an hour and each hour like a day. Aside from when the first meal was brought around, I didn't see anybody until the second meal, with one officer opening my trap a few minutes before to conduct a check, which I assumed was for some sort of count. I could hear the traps on either side of my cell opening and closing with the same interval in between, aside from a couple when someone complained about remaining locked inside.

"It's up to the governor," was all I heard one officer call back to someone's question, followed by an enormous thud as some unhappy inmate kicked their door. What the hell had I gotten myself into?

The first full day inside a prison cell was literally hell, a slow torture pulling me through each agonising second at a time. The torture wasn't physical, of course. This place wasn't designed to test a person physically, not unless they got caught up in some physical altercation with another prisoner. No, this place tested the very limits of a person's mental capacity, and that was torture enough. The endless noise, cycling through shouting, banging on doors, laughing, more abuse, more banging on doors, the conversations held under the doors between different cells, more banging. It drove people mental.

For three days, I sat alone in my cell without a clue as to why we weren't allowed out. Those three days left me physically weak, the mental exhaustion of nerves and fear combining to suck all the strength out of me. The food didn't help, of course. It wasn't as if prison food had been designed with maximum nutritional value in mind. Some days, I went to sleep hungry, the serving barely enough to fill even my tiny stomach.

I tried to ask one of the officers when we would be allowed out, but he simply jammed the tray of food through the slot and told me he didn't have time for conversations. Someone a couple of cells down asked the same question, and the response was "Soon." And so, I continued sitting alone in that cell for three full days, wondering about some of the voices I could hear outside my door.

The funny thing is, those voices shared a lot of information with me. Their tone, volume, confidence, arrogance, conviction, every decibel acted like a tiny little indicator, each syllable adding another piece to a puzzle. I imagined those voices having faces and bodies, and identities. I heard names like Martha, Erica, Jess, and of course, the all-important Maddy. That one's voice I heard several times a day and always with definite arrogance, as if she were some kind of leader.

It wasn't until I was eventually let out along with the rest of the unit that I finally got to see those faces for myself. Three days after stepping into the cell, the door finally unlocked and slowly opened a wedge before stopping. The officer who unlocked it moved swiftly across the unit, unlocking the doors to cheers from those stuck inside. I felt something resembling the size and weight of a boat anchor drop into my middle with the realisation that all of my nightmarish thoughts during the past three days were about to come true.

I barely got to my feet when my door suddenly spun open, and in walked three women, the one in the lead barely slim enough to fit through the space. She had the kind of grin that you knew was trouble.

"Lee said you got something for me," she said and stopped just a couple of feet from me with her hand stretched out. I could see the officer through the doorway, unlocking doors directly opposite from my own, and I hesitated. The woman looked over her shoulder, and when she turned back to face me, her grin had widened enough to show teeth. "Don't worry about Cook. He's harmless." The other girls giggled.

"Maddie?"

"Who else did you expect?" the woman said and shot me a wink.

Trying to hide anything inside a tiny cell is virtually impossible, given the limited number of places on offer, and so I had kept the sock under my mattress, each day expecting an officer to come and search my room. Thankfully, it never happened. I bent down and pulled the corner of it up, then grabbed the sock and held it out to the woman. She snatched it out of my fingers without so much as a thank you and immediately turned towards the door. One of her friends gave me a careful up-and-down glance before following the others back out into the common area.

That had been my one-sided introduction to the woman who ran the unit, with her neither interested in me nor my name, just a sock that I assumed held some quantity of drugs.

"We're going to party today, girls," I heard her tell the others as she walked away, leaving me alone to figure things out on my own.

While I had washed myself in the sink a couple of times, what I craved the most was a shower, but not knowing the unwritten rules, I wasn't sure whether I could. It was during my final month of freedom that Ollie tried to prepare me as best he could for the inevitable reality we both knew I faced. He had served time himself, and so he shared as much as he could remember, every-thing from how to talk to people to how not to disrespect them. He said that respect was everything inside, and most of the violence usually happened due to someone disrespecting someone else.

Figuring I had no choice, and unable to hide behind a locked door anymore, I gripped every bit of courage I could muster, took a deep breath and headed out into the unit's common area. The dozens of voices sent chills through me as I imagined them all looking at me, checking out the latest arrival into their world and wanting to dissect me. All I could do was submit myself to the process and hope for the best. If that didn't work, then who knew how this would end for me?

CHAPTER 20

"Hey, look, it's a new girl," were the first words I heard someone shout from the far side of the unit, and when I looked over there, about a dozen faces turned in my direction, all wanting to see who the new arrival was. "Come and hang out with us," the same voice called out, and it took me a moment to identify the specific person. The girl in question stood amongst a group of about five others, the tallest one, and also the prettiest. She waved for me to come, and figuring I didn't have much of a choice, I did as she asked.

What really hit hardest for me was the overwhelming silence amongst the people standing on that side of the unit as they watched me approach. I could still hear the myriad of voices from the other end, with most of those inmates not interested in me at all. Perhaps it was because I had walked away from them that they turned their attention to something else. Not so those standing in front of me.

"What's your name?" the tall girl called out when I reached the edge of the corner of the landing. I could see more faces looking up at me from down on the ground level, although I found it much easier to ignore them by keeping my eyes up on our level.

"Emma," I called back and tried to force a weak smile. Someone giggled, and my cheeks just about exploded with colour.

The girl waited until I was close enough before she spoke again, this time lowering her voice enough to keep her words inside the circle of friends around her.

"I'm Tampa," she said, but didn't hold a hand out to shake. "This is Reggie, Phoenix, Sue." She pointed to each girl in turn, all except the last one, whom she made a special mention of. "And this cute little button is Lexie." I think the girl missed the five-foot mark by several inches. She stood just tall enough to reach the lower end of my armpit, and Tampa almost picked her up off the floor.

"Nice to meet you," I said, offering each girl a smile. Only Lexie reached out with a hand and shook with me, and I was surprised by how warm her hand was.

"So, watcha in for?" Tampa asked as she flicked her long black hair back over her shoulder.

When Ollie had prepped me during that month, he told me that one of the most common questions asked inside jail was what someone was in for. He said that the only ones who hesitated to answer were those with the kinds of charges other inmates frowned upon, charges that usually related to either anything to do with children or violence against women. He assured me that my charges weren't anything to worry about, but I still struggled to bring them up.

"S-s-someone got hurt at a party," was all I could bring myself to say initially, and I hated the way the words sounded when they rolled out of me. Nobody seemed to notice, though.

"You killed someone?" I looked at Lexie and shook my head, but then remembered the charge.

"It was an accident," I said. "Overdose."

That was when a couple of the girls nodded, as if knowing exactly what I meant. Even Tampa and Lexie exchanged a look that I didn't quite recognise. I wasn't sure whether it was a good thing or a bad thing and figured I'd find out in due course.

"She was my friend," I added and felt my top lip quiver.

"Oh, shit, I'm sorry," Tampa said and stepped closer with her arms held out. She pulled me in and gave me a hug, and the truth is, it felt so incredibly needed at that moment. I let out a sigh of relief and tightened my own arms around her until I felt her arms relax. When she pulled back again, she smiled.

"Sounds like what Sue here is going through." She pointed to the blonde girl standing next to me. "She got four years for crashing a car, and her friend died as well."

"Oh, I'm so sorry," I said, and offered another weak smile.

"How long did you get on the bottom?" Tampa asked.

"On the bottom?" It wasn't a term Ollie had shared with me, and I hated sounding like an absolute newbie.

"On the bottom," Tampa repeated. "As in non-parole period?"

"Oh, two years," I said. "I got four years total."

"That's four on top and two on the bottom," Sue said. "Exactly half of what I got. Damn lucky, if you ask me."

That was the first time I heard someone describe my guaranteed two years in prison as a lucky thing. It sure as hell didn't sound lucky to me, but when compared with Sue's sentence, I guess it was.

"Sue got four and eight," Lexie said. "And it's her first offence."

"You got eight years for a first offence?" I asked, almost dumbfounded.

"That's horrible."

"Who was your judge?" Tampa asked.

"Crookwell," I said, and a couple of the girls nodded in recognition.

"No wonder," Sue said. "Wish I got him instead of miserable old coot, Miller."

"Yeah, Miller is a hard arse," Tampa said. "You definitely got the pick of the bunch. I had Reynolds myself, but I made sure to let out a bit of cleavage, and he gave me three months." She laughed, as if her words somehow struck a humorous chord, one that nobody else reacted to.

"Bitch," I heard Lexie mumble, but Tampa heard her and leaned down with puckered lips.

"Don't be jealous, sweetie," she said with the biggest grin on her face. "You'll be out of here sooner than you think."

I don't know what happened, but the nerves, the anxiety I had been carrying around for days simply faded away over the course of those first few minutes. Somehow, I ended up blending in with that first group of girls, and it quickly became obvious that they weren't so different from me. We shared a lot of similarities, and I think that helped me mix in with the rest of them.

The conversation eventually turned to the reason for the lockdown, and all I had to do was stand back and listen as the girls lowered their voices to talk about the incident that shut down the unit. From what I could gather, a girl named Holly something or other had accumulated a significant drug debt with Maddie and ended up falling victim to a vicious attack carried out by three other girls. They attacked her in what was known as a dark zone where none of the building's surveillance cameras could reach.

The beating itself didn't involve weapons, from what I heard, but someone had taken things too far with a sustained and relentless kicking to the head of the victim. Lexie said she saw them wheel Holly out on a stretcher, unconscious, while Sue overheard an officer saying that she was in an induced coma. Tampa tried to confirm it with an officer who walked past our group, and he whispered the news that the victim had died.

For a moment, the girls stood silently staring at each other, their lips pursed together as if in shock. I tried to look just as empathic, but I didn't know the girl, so I felt a bit out of place when they started whispering to each other. I couldn't make out if any of them were actual friends with Holly, but as the news spread throughout the unit, I actually heard Maddie yell that *the bitch deserved what she got*, much to the shock of the girls standing around me.

"I need to go pee," Lexie eventually said and held a hand out to Tampa, who took it and followed her towards the corridor. The others looked at me with curiosity.

"Guess we had better give you the tour," Sue said, and I smiled with gratitude.

"That would be great," I said and let them lead me around the place.

The unit itself had three floors, with the cells running around the outside perimeter. The common area of the ground floor stood open, with the ceiling reaching all the way to the very top, some three storeys up. Sitting in the middle of that space were a bunch of tables with six round metal chairs attached to them. I could see some of them used for card games, others simply for conversation. Sue randomly introduced me to several people along the way. Some shook with me, others not. Two exposed staircases reached from the ground floor up to the first-floor landing that stretched around the inner walls. The guard rail consisted of four tubular pipes running around the edge of the landings, which a lot of the inmates leaned against as they watched whatever was happening on the ground level.

Phoenix pointed out the communal bathrooms on each floor, as well as the laundry, and the kitchenette, where inmates could make themselves hot drinks and stuff. They walked me around each of the floors in turn, sometimes pausing at a cell to introduce me to more people before continuing on. Most of the women appeared kind and receptive, with only the odd one looking at me with an attitude.

It wasn't until we reached Cell 3E that the mood changed within the group. Phoenix and Reggie had been leading the way, with Sue walking next to me. The door to that particular cell stood open, but none of the girls looked inside the way they had with virtually all of the previous ones. Figuring it best to follow their lead, I didn't look either, but the moment I passed the door, a familiar voice called out.

"Am I not good enough to be introduced to?"

Phoenix was the first to stop, and she turned to look back at Sue before rolling her eyes. I recognised the voice, of course. It wasn't hard to miss, considering how loud Maddie spoke with that authoritative croak of hers. Reggie looked at me with an apologetic smile, but I could tell none of them wanted to be there at that moment.

"No, of course not," Sue eventually said and motioned for me to follow her back to the door of the cell.

The cell had the same layout as my own, except for one thing. The bed had no top bunk, just a single mattress on which Maddie lay. Another girl knelt at the end of the mattress and appeared to be giving the woman a foot massage, or a rub at the very least. A third girl sat on a chair near the built-in desk, reading a magazine.

"Ah, Lee's little cat," she said, trying to make the words sound more like a mock. "What's your name, sweetie?"

"This is Emma," Sue said and immediately regretted it when Maddie glared at her with a look of death. "Sorry," Sue mouthed, looking at Reggie as she turned away.

"I'm Emma," I said, trying my best to sound enthusiastic, but it was obvious that this little meeting had nothing to do with getting acquainted. She ignored me completely, just like her friend Leona had during our initial meeting.

"And are you girls sharing all of our little rules to your new friend?" Maddie said as she inspected one of her nails.

"Yes, we are," Sue said, again taking the lead.

"Good," Maddie said. "Be sure to remind Tampa as well, especially the part about who is running this joint."

"Yes, of course," Sue said and motioned for me to leave with a subtle head tilt.

I couldn't get out of there quick enough, more than happy to leave the tension of that cell behind me. We barely got three or four doors up when Sue grabbed my arm and squeezed it with relief.

"Holy shit, I thought she was going to keep us in there forever," she whispered, looking behind us to make sure we weren't being followed.

"Keep walking," Reggie hissed as she passed us by, and I saw the girl who had been reading the newspaper walk out of the cell and approach us. She made eye contact with me, and there was no denying the chill that ran down my spine.

I considered myself a pretty good judge of character, and that girl scared me in a way I hadn't felt before. She wasn't exactly big, standing maybe five-seven or eight, her black hair trimmed down to almost a buzz cut save for the very top that hung down one side like an overgrown fringe. She wore a snake tattoo on the left side of her head that stretched down past her eye and around the back of her ear, with the snake's head facing the front of the girl's head. Both her arms displayed more tattoos, and there was no denying how intimidating she looked.

"That's Tash," Phoenix whispered once the girl had walked far enough not to hear how. "That assault on Holly?" I nodded. "She was one of the ones who beat the shit out of her."

I looked back at the girl as she continued walking along until she disappeared into a cell near the end, but not before taking a final look at where we stood. Another chill ran through me, and I wondered how much it would take to turn her into an enemy.

"Ah, I see you met Maddie's lapdog," Tampa said from behind me, not bothering to lower her voice. Lexie slapped her arm. "What?" Tampa asked.

"Careful, she'll hear you," Lexie hissed at her.

"So what?" Tampa said with arrogance while looking back at Maddie's open cell. "Let her."

That initial outing from my cell took just a couple of hours, but I swear I learnt more during those hours than I ever did during the subsequent months I spent inside. Those girls made sure to show me every possible thing I needed to know, introduced me to those inmates worth knowing, and even introduced me to a couple of officers whom they considered to be something of an asset.

Three of the four officers working the unit that day weren't what the girls considered useful, but the fourth one proved to be the exception. Tampa called him Merv the Perv, his name rhyming with the derogatory name she stuck him with, and I could see why. Even from a distance, it became apparent that the guy liked to watch the girls, especially those wearing uniforms that hugged their figures. Wanting to prove her point, Tampa tucked her shirt in tight enough to announce her bust to the world and then walked over to where the officer stood guard to ask him a question. His eye contact with her lasted about a second before we could see it dropped down to where they rested between her cleavage. When Tampa thanked him and turned to walk back to where we stood, his eyes immediately zeroed in on her butt and remained there until she turned the corner of the walkway.

The girls told me that each shift had at least one officer who would always go above and beyond to appease the prisoners. A couple of the girls didn't flinch when admitting that they used sexual advances for special privileges, with one admitting that she performed acts on Merv the Perv a few times. The others giggled at the prospect, but Phoenix insisted she had given him some grip satisfaction once or twice.

When the day eventually ended and I ended up back in my cell with the door closed, I wasn't sure whether to feel relieved, sad, or hang onto my nerves. While I had made a few friends, so to speak, I still hadn't overcome the initial apprehension about the place. It felt like danger lurked around every corner, and I couldn't get the look that Tash had given me, a girl who some called a long-termer.

Natasha Russell killed her stepdad when she was just fourteen years old after suffering years of abuse. Now aged in her early thirties, she had spent the majority of her life in and out of prison. Perhaps she was one of those prisoners some called institutionalised, who were more comfortable inside than outside. It didn't take much to cross her kind, and I had no doubt that if Maddie gave her the order, she wouldn't hesitate to come for me. What I didn't know was that she would come at me for another reason, one I hadn't fully considered.

CHAPTER 21

I think I settled into prison life better than I had expected, with the days becoming more of a routine than anything. Each morning began in much the same way, with the unit officers first checking each cell for their morning count, before unlocking us around eight o'clock, at which point some of the inmates headed off to work, while the rest remained in the unit to do as they pleased.

The prison itself had six units altogether, each one housing between sixty and eighty inmates. Each unit stood around a large rectangular area called the *Yard*, a concreted space containing a basketball court, an outdoor gym, and a bunch of seats that rose up like the kind of bleachers you'd see at a sports field. The top step was where Maddie and her closest allies sat during our unit's time in the yard, overlooking the inmates like some sort of military general.

I couldn't get any work placement during those first few months. The opportunities were very limited, and a person could only get one by either knowing someone who could whisper into the ear of a supervisor or by an inmate leaving the job and making way for a replacement. That meant I had to go out into the yard with the rest of the unit each day and spend two hours either walking around or hanging out with girls with whom I had built up a relationship. The problem I had was that there weren't that many of them.

Eight weeks after I arrived at the prison, Tampa earned an early release and bid each of us farewell. Three days later, news came back that she was dead, killed in some random mugging that had all the hallmarks of a hit. I still remember Maddie's heartless cackle when she first heard the news, and Trixie jumping off the bed to race to the woman's cell for God knows what. Thankfully, Phoenix and I were able to restrain her enough to hold her back. Who knows what would have happened if she had actually made it across the unit?

The rumour was that Maddie had paid one of her friends to take care of Tampa. According to Reggie, she had quite a number of girls on the outside willing to do her bidding, thanks to her sizable inheritance. Maddie's father had struck it lucky with some stocks back in the early eighties and left her quite a large sum of money. Her son remained her primary contact on the outside and, with access to her fortune, never shied away from helping his mother spend it.

Tampa's death hit everybody hard, including me. She had been the first person inside who actually made me feel part of something, even if it was inside a disgusting and dishevelled prison unit. She had always been kind and caring, almost mothering the rest of us, despite being just a couple of years older than me. She had that kind of maternal instinct that others just seemed to gravitate towards.

Lexie took her death the hardest, not only because they shared a cell together, but because she had known Tampa on the outside. The pair attended the same schools and had known each other since kindergarten. We're talking lifelong friends torn apart because of another woman's bitterness. Maddie never came right out and said that she was responsible for Tampa's death, but she didn't need to. Most of us knew without the confession. Unfortunately,

Lexie wasn't willing to let it go and constantly talked about getting her revenge.

For me, the hardest part of the day would always be the yard for a straightforward reason. It was the one time of the day when the others weren't around, and I would end up spending those two hours walking around the perimeter of the yard pretending to exercise. Both Phoenix and Lexie worked in the kitchen, while Reggie had a job in the infirmary, or the medical unit, if you will. Sue remained in the unit as she worked as the unit billet and so had her own assigned jobs. That left me to face the prospect of being alone with Maddie and her taunting brigade to use me for their own amusement.

Perhaps the silver lining for me was the cell situation. During those first three months, I think I had four cellmates come and go, all within a matter of days from each other. Joan, the first, came a week after me and left the very next day, after a violent altercation with Tash. Next came Bec, a former nun who got busted for heroin trafficking, if you can believe it. She stayed almost a week, but then got moved to Bravo Unit to make way for Zionara, an African girl who didn't last a single day. She had barely unpacked her belongings before she went completely ballistic in the cell. Thankfully, the doors hadn't been locked, or who knows what would have happened to me.

The last of the four and the one who stayed the longest was Tilly. She was the reason the whole nasty business with Tash came about, and not in the way you expect. Here's the thing. Either through my own ignorance or because I'm not into girls, I completely missed all of the warning signs the others repeatedly pointed out to me. They kept saying that Tash had a thing for me, that they could see the lust in her eyes while she watched me from afar. I honestly thought they were nothing more than jokes until the business with Tilly brought it to the forefront.

Tilly also had a thing for me, although she didn't hide it the way Tash did. This girl came right out with it the moment she laid eyes on me, her flirtatious comments constantly thrown my way.

"Better sleep with your eyes open, cupcake," is what she used to say whenever she climbed onto her bed. She'd wink at me and smile, before wishing me sweet dreams. It got so bad that I stopped using the toilet completely during lockdown hours, for fear of her trying something while I had my pants down.

The mistake Tilly made was openly bragging about wanting to get into my panties. She would whistle at me whenever I passed by on the floor of the unit, and she would constantly stare at me when out in the yard. Her attention continued every minute of the day, and it honestly exhausted me. And while I tried my best to ignore it, someone else was doing her best to look out for it, letting the jealousy build up until it reached explosive levels.

Tilly wasn't always so bad. There were times while we were locked in the cell that she could be quite friendly, in a non-aggressive kind of way. She had done time at St. Agnes herself, and we could talk for hours about the place, with Sister Celia coming up more often than not. I guess you could say that the nun had built herself quite a reputation with her aggressive attitude and, in a way, became the face of the place whenever people talked about it.

What surprised me the most was how Tilly told me that she was one of the few people whom Sister Celia actually took a liking to.

"There was this one time where she took me back into her office and flipped through an old photo album. There weren't many pictures of her as a child, but those I did see definitely showed one happy kid," Tilly told me. "She grew up on a farm up near Wrexham, where she rode horses from an early age. Can you believe that? A horse-loving nun."

I tried to imagine Sister Celia on a horse and couldn't. There was just something about that frown that wouldn't quite gel with such a beautiful animal. No matter how much I tried to picture her as a child, the image of the woman yelling at me for sneaking out to watch a movie is one I couldn't get past. Maybe it was because of my own past that I couldn't picture her as anything but an angry woman. It didn't matter, of course. This is about Tilly more than Sister Celia, and while those talks might have been nice for brief moments in time, they didn't go anywhere near enough to erase the rest of her behaviour.

One day in early July, I found myself out in the yard with the rest of my unit. Sue had been granted permission to come out with us on account of her having not been out of the unit in more than a week, and one of the officers agreed for her to swap shifts with another girl. It was a beautiful day, the sky about as blue as you could imagine, without a single hint of clouds anywhere. It wasn't overly hot, but the girls in the yard still insisted on taking off as much of their clothing as permitted without the officers on duty flipping out.

I saw Tash standing in the shade on top of the bleachers during our first lap around the walking track, Sue walking at an elevated pace to build up her heart rate. She offered to run alone, but I didn't want to go through another session on my own, so I had promised to join her if we could make it a quick walk instead of a slow run. Sue agreed, which immediately eased my anxiety, but not entirely.

You'd think I would get used to it after spending all those weeks alone, but to be honest, it doesn't get any easier just because you've been through it a few times. For me, each day alone in that yard brought new challenges my way, and I needed to find new ways to deal with them. I'm fairly certain Maddie used me as her own private piece of amusement, continuously watching me as her minions tried to make my life a living hell for no logical reason other than entertainment. Some days, I could see her call out commands to those down on ground level, while other times, she'd lean in close to someone near her and whisper to them instead.

The end result was always the same, though. Someone would unintentionally run into me on the track and knock me to the ground, or a random ball would fly straight at my face. Some days, those balls would connect and send the yard into fits of laughter; other days, they would miss, only for several attempts to be made. Like I said, it was nothing more than entertainment.

Don't get me wrong, I made several friends outside of my usual circle as well, but the problem was that Maddie got to each and every one of them, her intimidation enough to push them away from me. The only one who ever ignored Maddie's threat tactics was a lady named Raelene something or other, and she spent three days walking around the yard with me. I was beginning to think that maybe the tide had turned when I saw Maddie's usual minions focus their attention on another girl in the yard, but as it turned out, that had only been a diversionary tactic.

When the attack came, I barely noticed. One second, Raelene was walking beside me, talking about how she only had another four sleeps to go before she could walk through her favourite park again, and the next, I found myself a couple of dozen steps ahead and her lying on the ground in a growing pool of blood. The stabbing happened in the blink of an eye, the attacker bumping into her ever so subtly. Raelene didn't cry out at all, which was why I continued on completely unaware.

That had been the first time I saw just how seriously Maddie took her role as unit leader. She didn't take kindly to having her orders ignored and made it frightfully clear that she was in charge. Thankfully, the blade missed all of her vital organs and major arteries, but she did spend two weeks in a nearby hospital and was eventually released directly from there. It came as no surprise to me that I never heard from her again, but I was also grateful. No contact from a living person was much better than no contact due to death.

My anxiety didn't disappear as I hated the thought of Sue ending up hurt, as Raelene did. I knew Maddie was more than capable of ordering a hit on Sue, and my friend assured me she would be OK, but that still didn't make things any easier for me. Each time I heard some shouting or felt someone get too close to us, my insides would tighten and I'd nervously look around to try and spot the threat. Sue wanted to ease my mind by keeping the conversation flowing, but my eyes couldn't be averted by the conversation alone.

The first hour went by without incident that morning. In fact, Maddie wasn't in her usual seat atop the bleacher seats, which was one of the main reasons my nerves had eased considerably. With another beautiful afternoon for us weatherwise, I enjoyed the heat from the sunshine and imagined myself sitting on the beach at Bexhill, with Jack and Ollie sitting either side of me as we sunned ourselves. Don't get me wrong, I liked Sue and appreciated her presence, but nothing compares to the company of people you consider family.

When it finally happened, I had paused briefly to close my eyes and turn my face up towards the sun. Sue had just mentioned that she also loved the beach and wish she could have been lying on a towel with sunglasses on and just listening to the sound of the ocean, which was why I thought of the summer we spent at Bexhill. An ear-splitting scream suddenly exploded just a few feet from me, and when I opened my eyes and looked, I saw Tilly lying on the ground as flashbacks of Raelene flooded my brain. I took a couple of nervous steps backwards as I stared at the lifeless eyes of a girl I had earlier wished good luck with a phone call to her mother.

I didn't see Tash standing nearby until she took a couple of steps towards me, and even then, I completely missed the makeshift blade dangling beside her leg. She had a kind of empathic look on her face, a vague smile that had absolutely no malice behind it. The way she looked at me reminded me of how Jack once looked at me during a moment of weakness, when his true feelings came to the surface.

In the blink of an eye, Tash suddenly dropped the shank to the ground, held her hands up and then interlaced the fingers on top of her head as she knelt. A couple of armed officers with their pistols pointed at Tash called for her to freeze and get down on the ground.

"I saved you," was all Tash whispered to me before she lay face down on the concrete.

The shank Tilly was going to use to stab me lay underneath her, with just a small portion of the handle sticking out from under her back. People later told me that she had been venting her jealousy to a couple of other girls and only flipped out when someone suggested Sue and me were a couple. That someone? Maddie's minion, Flo. Maddie wanted to stoke the fire and create some more entertainment, but then got called to the governor's office for an unrelated matter.

Tash turned out to be the biggest surprise of all. While she happily followed Maddie's orders most of the time, she refused when it came to me. As it turned out, Tash had quite a thing for me and hated the idea of Maddie repeatedly torturing me. When she heard that she had sent Tilly to stab me out in the open yard, Tash took it upon herself to stop the attack by taking out Tilly once and for all, more so because she didn't want to risk us getting locked in a cell together.

I genuinely believe that Tash, the one person whom I had feared would one day come calling for me, saved my life that day, just as she said she did. In a single act of unselfish kindness, she murdered a girl for a complete stranger in full view of the cameras and earned herself an additional life sentence. We hadn't exchanged a single word other than the ones she whispered to me after killing Tilly, and yet she sacrificed her life to save mine.

CHAPTER 22

While I did suffer quite a bit those first few months, in so many different ways, life did eventually become that routine I mentioned before. The thing about routine is that it takes away the unpredictability of prison, and routine is what helps pass the time. Unfortunately for me, there's another tool people use to pass the time, and it also helps considerably with anxiety, fear, depression, boredom, and anything else you struggle with. Want to know what it is? Drugs.

I know I have been making out that I'm a victim of the system, and down on my luck, and suffered a gross injustice being sent to prison in the first place, but maybe I have been overplaying that card a little too much. I'm not the goody-two-shoes I try to make myself out to be. I guess this honesty thing is harder than I imagined, and I'd better tell you about the parts I conveniently skipped.

While prison might have been one way for many to escape the miserable existence of the streets by offering a roof and three meals a day, for me, it only amplified the reality of who I was...or rather *what* I was...an addict. Prisons limited the availability of certain drugs, but there was always something to use, although the costs for using them also went up considerably. Reggie proved to be the primary source for our group, the one who had the right contacts with the outside world and the means to smuggle those drugs into the prison. Giving grip service to specific guards helped a lot, as did having a brother who knew how to manipulate those same guards in other ways.

On the street, I usually preferred to go for heroin, but inside, beggars couldn't be choosers. I went with whatever was available, even if it meant swallowing a pill someone had already half-digested. For the right price, you could persuade people to do just about anything, including selling their medication, which is where the unit economy really boomed. Half the inmates paid the other half for their meds, and then used that money to buy other drugs whenever they made it into the building.

I remember the night when I first revealed my secret to Jack, and the look of utter shock as he watched me pull the syringe from the make-shift pouch I used to conceal my drugs. You cannot imagine how bad I felt when I offered him that first hit, knowing just how much he was against using them. He had lost his mother because of them, and her death subsequently changed the course of his life, one that guaranteed him years of struggling. A true friend would never have offered him that hit, or so I told myself for a long time after that night.

Offering Jack drugs wasn't the only guilt I carried around with myself. I had done plenty of bad things that reminded me I wasn't such a perfect person. Becoming a full-blown addict without Jack ever finding out proved to be just the start in a long line of secrets and bad decisions I brought into my life. Prostitution, stealing, lying, too many bad things to mention. Yes, I could keep telling myself that I did them all to survive, but where does a person draw a line and finally end the vicious cycle?

Survival can be used as an excuse for sure, but can you still use it when more desirable alternatives exist? I should know because I had plenty of alternative options growing up. Find yourself hungry? Go to the nearest charity store, food bank, or even a church. Someone is always able to point you in the right direction. Need a place to stay? The city is literally brimming with shelters and halfway houses that offer support to minors. Drugs to cope? Endless counselling services and support services open their doors daily. Already hooked? Plenty of programs on offer. All I had to do was choose one. And yet I didn't choose any of them.

I used prostitution as an excuse for needing money to help with food and shelter, and yet I used most of it to buy drugs. I used drugs to escape my reality, often funding friends just so I had someone to share the experience with. Sometimes, the thing I wanted to escape the most proved to be the one thing I couldn't run away from...me, and that's where the cycle of abuse and neglect continued to permeate my entire life.

That first prison sentence was supposed to rehabilitate me, or so the counsellors and politicians used to say. We had access to courses designed to help us gain job qualifications through various classes, but also teach us about the value of holding steady employment. Most of the women who joined those courses did so to use them to help boost their chances of getting parole. If they were seen to be actively trying to better themselves, then they were considered less of a threat to society.

I did do one course during that first stretch, a five-day Barista course. I hated every minute of it, from listening to the annoying instructor to the smell of the coffee itself. Yes, I'm one of those freakish people who doesn't drink coffee, or tea for that matter. I guess I just never got used to the taste. I honestly thought I wasn't going to make it, and I almost dropped out halfway through, but I ended up pushing through when Phoenix told me to. Having her sitting beside me helped as well.

The significant change to my routine came four days after the new year when someone got fired from the kitchen for stealing some sugar. She had scooped a handful into a plastic bag and hid it between her butt cheeks and would have gotten away with it were it not for one of the female officers spotting her slip the pouch into the back end of her pants. One inspection later, the bag reappeared in the palm of the inmate's hand as she handed it over, and her job as a dishwasher became mine.

I had jobs in my life before, of course, but that one changed me. In a weird kind of way, that kitchen job gave me purpose in a way that no other position ever had. A prison kitchen is perhaps one of the two most important places for any inmate, with the medical wing being the other. I think it was Lexie who once told me that you never messed with an inmate's food or pills, no matter what. They were the two things that made an inmate's day, and they would fight tooth and nail to get them.

Kitchen shifts were split into two across the day, with the first shift starting at five in the morning until noon, and the afternoon shift starting at noon and finishing at seven. The morning crew took care of breakfast and lunch, with the afternoon crew taking care of dinner, as well as prepping for the next day. I ended up on the afternoon shift, along with Phoenix.

Two different dishwashers worked in the kitchen, with each of us responsible for two stations. I took the saucepans and trays, which came to me via this convenient conveyor belt, and I would scrub each one by hand in a huge sink filled with soapy water. I then hung them from metal hooks on these drying racks, gave them a quick rinse with a hose and then wheeled the trolley into the corner once it was full. I had to take care of twelve racks in all, and each held about ten when full, so you can imagine the sheer number of items I had to scrub clean each cycle. Add to that various other duties as dictated by the civilian cooks, and it made for a busy day.

While I didn't care much for the actual work, the reason I appreciated the job so much is that it gave me what I normally used the drugs for. As long as I was busy, I found my mind barely finding the time to think about stuff. With the music blaring across the kitchen and several conversations consisting of humour and random stories keeping us occupied, those bitter voices from my past barely made an appearance most days, and by the time night came, I was too tired to care.

If I thought the days rolled by before that job, it was nothing compared to my time after getting into the kitchen. I began to feel more and more like a member of society, even if that society consisted of serious criminals existing solely behind the walls of a prison. I worked a job just like anybody doing the same on the outside, a job with responsibilities, a wage, a timetable, and a purpose. Unlike any of the previous jobs I had worked, this one felt so much more important, its purpose very real. Unlike being a fashion show runner, where I always felt like I was just playing games, this job served an actual purpose, one appreciated by every person living in the jail.

The biggest benefit I found didn't occur to me for almost a month after getting the job, but when it did, I think it offered me the first real insight into the possibilities. I began to notice my cravings for drugs fading away. It wasn't easy, of course, and I did end up on a methadone program to ease my withdrawal symptoms, but I could sense that maybe life without drugs might just be possible. That kitchen job gave me the kind of purpose that acted like a kind of distraction, one that kept my urges at bay.

Don't get me wrong, it wasn't always smooth sailing. There were some days I couldn't even get out of bed because of the pain, and I did slip back into the habit a number of times as well, but that small glimmer of hope was what I remembered most. If only I had focused on that part of it, perhaps I might have transitioned faster than I did, but like I said before, fairytales rarely come true in this life and for me, that small glimmer of hope eventually disappeared, and a much darker shadow rolled across my world again.

I worked the kitchen job for almost fourteen months before my demons came calling for me, and I ended up getting fired for stealing. It wasn't the first time I had smuggled coffee back to the unit, but it was the first time the officers caught me. I had been stealing various items over the course of the previous couple of months, at first selling them for money that I used to buy normal shopping items, but then eventually to fund the habit that I never quite entirely left behind.

The event that pushed me over the edge and back into the arms of whatever drugs I could get my hands on was hearing the news that Ollie had gotten himself arrested again and ended up with a three-year sentence for armed robbery. Jack told me our friend collapsed to the floor during sentencing and had to be carried out by the courtroom security. We both cried during that visit, Jack because of him seeing me break down, and me because I knew the struggle Ollie would face, given that he held the darkest demons of all.

I hit the drugs hard, those first few months after his sentencing, and ignored all prospects of a job. My friendships also began to fizzle out, thanks to me preferring to remain alone, for the sake of saving anyone close to me of facing Maddie's continuing threats. She still used me for her own sick entertainment as much as possible, but I had gotten so used to it, I barely noticed it anymore. Most days, I was so high, I barely cared about anything at all anymore. Life had managed to suck every bit of energy out of me and I no longer cared about the past, present, or future.

CHAPTER 23

On Wednesday, the 7th of March, the door to my cell opened and two officers called my name, beckoning me to grab my bag and follow them. It was an event I had pictured a million different ways during the previous two years and always felt like it would be a moment of celebration for me, the event something of a victory, and yet when it finally happened, it felt anything but a win. The last thing I expected when I finally walked out of the place was to feel depressed, and yet that's exactly what happened.

Just two short years was all it took for my life to feel unravelled entirely in a way I had never experienced before. Before coming into prison, I felt like I had a purpose, with friends and somewhat of a family, even if they weren't exactly blood. I had a job, a schedule, places to be, and parties to enjoy. When I walked out of prison, I had neither a job nor a purpose, a home that felt like I was going backwards, and a habit I knew I had no chance of beating.

It wasn't as if I had no friends. Jack came and picked me up from the front of the prison in his car and drove me around to the halfway house, which the prison support service had booked me into. We're talking the mirror image of Blackrock, except this new place didn't have juniors like the original had. The youngest were eighteen, and almost the entire population of the building had issues of some kind, from drug or alcohol addiction, battling some deadly disease, or just trying to deal with the mental demons we all seemed to carry around with us.

The first thing that stood out to me about Logan House was the eerie similarity to my previous home at Blackrock, my room also on the same floor. The room didn't quite match up to the other one, but I wasn't about to complain to anybody about having a room to myself. It had been a long time since I had the benefit of some alone time, including access to my very own bathroom. After spending almost two years needing to pee with someone else in the room, it definitely felt exhilarating to be able to take care of my business in privacy.

The other significant difference between Logan's and Blackrock is that security didn't seem to care about who we had in our room. While there was a guard sitting in the office when I first arrived, he barely looked up from his phone when I handed him the envelope containing my placement. He peered into the top of the open envelope, then grabbed a key, pointed me in the general direction of a linen cupboard, told me to take a pack, and pointed to where the stairs took me up to my floor.

"Is there someone I should see up there?" I asked, remembering how we had to visit the supervisor at Blackrock, but the guard shook his head and waved me away as if I had interrupted his day. Jack rolled his eyes at me when I looked at him and motioned for us to leave.

Jack ended up staying with me that first night, and when we got hungry around five, he offered to head out and pick us up a pizza. I wasn't about to turn down the first proper take-out meal in two years and asked for one with everything on it.

"One with the lot coming right up," he said with a grin and kissed me on the top of my head.

Once he was gone, I went to the window and waited for him to appear in the car park and once I saw his car disappear a few minutes later, a sudden rush of guilt rushed through me as I headed for the door. The lies which I had promised myself to leave behind hadn't quite finished with me, and it wasn't until that moment that I realised just how much of a hold they had on me.

It took me just five minutes to find what I was looking for, the second girl I walked into in the corridor, pointing me to a door at the very end. I knocked on it once, and when it opened, I held up a wad of notes that immediately got me inside. A few seconds later, I walked out a bit poorer, financially wise, but prepped to revisit an old friend, one I hadn't seen in quite some time.

I didn't even blink when I got back to my room, went into the bathroom and locked the door just in case Jack came back quicker than expected. Despite it being a weeknight, the pizza would still need to cook, and that alone should have given me at least thirty minutes to play with. I didn't even need half that time. That first shot hit me faster than a freight train, the effects rushing through me in a wave of relief as an old friend came home. I sat on the toilet lid with my eyes closed for ages, just letting that buzz engulf me until I heard Jack calling out that he had returned.

When I came out of the bathroom, I met Jack's gaze for just the briefest of moments, but it was enough to tell me that he knew exactly what I had been up to. Despite us both doing our best to ignore each other's reactions, there was no hiding my look of shame nor his look of disappointment. He knew what I had done, and I knew that he knew, and that was all there was to it.

Since I didn't have a television, we ate mostly in silence, with just the noise of distant voices from out in the hallway. I kept saying how good the pizza tasted, and Jack kept telling me that he didn't have fast food anywhere near as much as he used to, but that was about the extent of our conversation. There was no getting away from that uncomfortable silence which took up the gaps in between those meaningless comments.

The most uncomfortable part of the evening came when we finished the pizza and ran out of things to say, namely because I wanted to focus on my high, and Jack looked as if he would rather have been getting a root canal. I felt bad for him, mainly because it had been my shooting up that brought on that uncomfortable silence between us. Who knows how things might have played out if I had stayed clean for just a day? Then again, hindsight isn't exactly anybody's friend.

"I saw Ollie yesterday," Jack told me when it felt like nothing was going to break that silence, and I seized on the comment.

"Oh, really? How is he?"

"Bad," Jack said. "He looks like he's aged about a decade since I last saw him, and he had this bruise on the side of his face."

"Somebody's beating on him?"

"He wouldn't say," Jack said as he poured himself another glass of Coke. "He got very uncomfortable when I asked him about it, and I figured it was best just to let it go."

"I'm going to see him tomorrow," I said. "It feels like I haven't seen him in so long."

"You haven't," Jack said, and he was right. I hadn't seen my friend in more than a year, and it hurt, more so than Jack understood.

Just as a parent isn't supposed to have a favourite child, the same can be said about friendships like ours. Jack and Ollie were my family, and the three of us shared a bond closer than most siblings, one that couldn't be dissected and compared. They were just…family…and each one of them brought their own unique personality to the table. Did *I* have a favourite? Not in the context you might think, but I did certainly have more in common with one over the other.

When I get right down to the inner workings of our friendships, I would have to say that I'm closer to Jack, but only by the smallest of margins. He never judged me and always brought the best advice whenever I needed a shoulder to lean on. He knew me better than I knew myself, and just had that paternal side to him that I respected so much.

Ollie, however, shared way too many similarities with me, including some of the worst traits imaginable. He knew better than Jack about the struggles with drugs, having battled those demons only slightly longer than I had. It was also Ollie who seemed to struggle with the same types of social issues, preferring isolation over inclusion. Ollie found it more comfortable hiding away in a locked room for days, like me, while Jack would rather be in a crowd during those darker days.

The thing is, both of them brought something different to the table, which was why I needed them both. Not just needed them, but damn near relied on them. I couldn't imagine living my life without either one, which was why the eventual events that engulfed us hurt so badly. I told you before that fairytales rarely come true in our world, and the three of us were no different. Sooner or later, destiny or fate or whatever you want to call it would pay us a visit, and that would be when the harsh reality of life came calling.

"You want me to take you to see him?" Jack asked when he finished his drink, and I shook my head.

"I'd rather go and see him alone," I said. "No offence, but we haven't seen each other in so long, I think it might be best." Jack looked at me and held his hands out.

"Since when do you take offence to you having choices?" he asked, and I smiled, then held out an arm for him to lean in.

We hugged, and when it didn't immediately end with Jack pulling back, I pulled him in a little closer and tightened my hold on him. It felt good in a way I cannot describe. It wasn't sexual at all, not even vaguely erotic, but his touching me like that reminded me of who he was. This wasn't just some guy whom I could hop into bed with at any time and use for a bit of relief. No, this was someone far too valuable to risk for such a fractional moment. What I held in my arms felt like a piece of me, a part of my life, and something I needed to protect at all costs, just like Jack would protect me.

We must have sat on the couch like that for almost an hour before the room fell into complete darkness, and it was then that I moved just enough for the subtle message to pass between us. Jack let go and moved back, but before he got too far, I reached out and grabbed his hand.

"Stay with me tonight," I whispered, the thought of him leaving suddenly too hard to deal with. I had yearned for a night in so long, and now that I had the chance, I couldn't think of anything worse. I needed him, not as a lover, or even a friend, but as something much deeper than that. I wanted to feel safe, protected, and able to sleep without wondering whether I would wake up with a shank in my throat, or wake up at all, for that matter.

"Of course I'll stay," Jack said without hesitation and without even questioning why, he followed me into the bedroom where we lay fully dressed on top of the covers and spooned, him behind me with his arms curled around me.

I can't tell you how long we lay like that because I'm fairly certain I fell asleep like that within seconds. Nothing interrupted that night, not the need to pee, or bad dreams. From the moment I fell asleep, I fell into a state of deep rest, all of my anxieties and problems vanishing in an instant. While I couldn't say that I had finally come home, it did feel somewhat of a homecoming, made possible by one of the closest friends I ever had.

CHAPTER 24

One of the most common misconceptions I've heard about prison is that people will do anything to stay out of the place. For some people, that idea couldn't have been further from the truth. Being institutionalised isn't just about being inside for a great many years and becoming so used to the rules and routine that you find it near impossible to make a decision on your own. Or not to me, at least.

I knew girls barely twenty-five years old who you could consider institutionalised, and not because of how much time they've spent inside. What those girls benefited from the most was the sheer fact that they were looked after by a system, the same system that adopted me at four months old and subsequently shipped me from one home to the next while trying to find something that fit.

What those girls got used to wasn't just the routine, but the idea that they would have somewhere to sleep, would have three square meals a day, and access to everything from medical care to toiletries. They got to sidestep commitments like paying the rent, the utilities, and budgeting for everyday needs. They didn't have to worry about price rises, or transportation needs, or looking for work just to survive. Those girls needed to have their lives taken care of by that system, and so for many of them, prison felt like a refuge rather than a deterrent.

I didn't see myself as one of those girls. Yes, I had been part of that system my entire life, well, *almost* my entire life, but I still knew and recognised how much freedom meant. I liked the idea of deciding what I wanted to eat for each meal. I liked the freedom to be able to walk out of my front door and decide which direction to walk, which bus to catch, and what supermarket to buy my groceries. To me, prison took away the things that differentiated me from everyone else in the building. It stole a person's identity and turned them into a number that had to conform to a set of rules and regulations, a timetable for each and every day, and share the same kind of existence as a hundred other women. Or at least that's what I thought.

When I opened my eyes the following morning to Jack moving around, I could tell the sun hadn't quite come up yet, with the dawn of a new day still in progress. My eyes felt heavy, and I struggled to open them, but I felt refreshed and ready to start a new chapter in my life. He smiled down at me when he saw me slowly stretching.

"Sorry. Did I wake you?"

"I wanted to get up anyway," I said. "Need to get things happening."

"I have to get to work early. I promised Brett that I'd open up this morning."

"That's cool," I said and swung my legs onto the floor. Five minutes later, I gave Jack a parting hug at the door, felt him kiss the top of my forehead before he disappeared into the day. I closed the door and considered falling back into bed, but I knew I wouldn't get up again if I did.

What I didn't tell Jack was that it hadn't been him who woke me up that morning, although it was because of him that I opened my eyes. The truth was that my body clock, my prison body clock, always woke me up at the crack of dawn, just so I would be ready to go when the officers came around to collect the early morning workers, since my latest cellmate was one. It's funny how I hated being awake when there was someone else in the cell with me, but I truly enjoyed my alone time when they weren't. Sleeping while alone in the cell just felt like a waste, and so I preferred to be awake.

The other reason I wanted to get up early was because I wanted to stick to my original plan of visiting Ollie, and having rejected Jack's offer to drive me, I had to find my own way, which, for a person low on funds and without wheels, meant the bus or the train. Given the distance to the prison, I figured about two hours each way, and I wanted to get there mid-morning at the very latest. If my prison was anything to go by, entry wasn't always guaranteed, and neither was the efficiency to make it happen fast. Jack often told me it took him a couple of hours just getting processed inside, so for someone coming by public transport, that had the potential to blow out to an entire day. Seeing Ollie was worth the effort, of course, but that didn't mean I had to enjoy the journey getting there.

My first stop once I showered and got myself looking half presentable was a bakery I found a couple of blocks from Logan's front door. The pizza did the job the previous evening, but I woke up almost shaking from low blood sugar, and it took a couple of freshly-baked rolls to get me going again—that and a large bottle of double-espresso iced coffee. The sweetness alone satisfied me, but that underlying bitterness of the coffee seriously gave my system a buzz.

With Pentonville sitting on the other side of the map, I ended up catching two trains and a bus to get there, a good thing since Ollie was due to be moved to another prison in the coming days, located further out in the country. We're talking a compass and a cut lunch kind of trip to visit him, and one I would definitely need Jack and his car for. Despite leaving the flat just before seven, I didn't reach the prison entrance until almost eleven and immediately felt my heart sink when I saw the line waiting to get inside. At one point, I considered turning around and heading back home, but then I heard someone call out something about an information tour, and more than half the line suddenly disappeared down a side door.

I have to admit that I didn't feel at ease walking into another prison so soon after walking out of my own. Call it getting triggered, or having flashbacks, my insides felt completely unsettled as I stood in that foyer watching uniformed officers processing those standing ahead of me. It felt like I had gone back in time. I was actually worried that someone would recognise me and point the escapee out to the others.

"Quick, grab her, she's not supposed to be out," one would yell and then his mates would rush at me before throwing me to the floor."

"Miss, I need your ID," the lady behind the counter repeated with frustration, pulling me from my dreamlike distraction.

"Sorry," I said, pulled my purse from the handbag and held out my card, which the officer snatched.

Pleasantries were completely optional when it came to prison officers, and the woman who signed me in didn't care for them, or so it seemed. Maybe she could sense what I was. Either that, or the system flagged my recent release, which was why she gave me that standard sideways glance with added judgment.

"Over to the scanner," she said, pointing to where one of her colleagues was in the middle of explaining the way through a scanning machine to another woman. And then, not bothering to wait for me to move, she tilted her head sideways and shouted to the person behind me. "NEXT."

For the next ten minutes, I subjected myself to an X-ray scanning machine, a physical pat down by another female officer, and an escort through to where the rest of the visitors stood waiting for the next walk to the visiting room. There must have been a group of about twenty people, with just enough seating for ten. I stood near the back, a good thing as the front few looked cramped into a corner.

Another officer eventually turned up and, after instructing us to keep close, he opened the gate and showed us through into a lit-up corridor. Five minutes later, I found myself inside a large room with multiple tables and chairs where several visitors had already taken their seats. Another queue formed in front of a small desk, and when I reached the front, another officer directed me to a specific table in the right rear corner of the room.

It was after taking a seat that I suddenly felt extremely uncomfortable, with more flashbacks tormenting me. Visits were perhaps one of the most challenging times for me, mainly because of how hard it was to leave loved ones behind at the end of the visit. Or should that be them leaving me behind? I couldn't remember any visit feeling normal for me. The end was what always plagued me before it had even begun. I know how it sounds, but it was another form of self-sabotage that I struggled to control.

When Ollie finally appeared, walking into the room amongst a group of inmates, I almost felt unable to stand. His appearance took me by complete surprise. Jack had told me he looked bad, and I didn't quite understand *how* bad. His face had turned gaunt, the defined cheekbones sticking out like uncomfortable protrusions. His eyes sat way too deeply and looked almost closed as he approached me.

"Damn, it's good to see you," a croaky voice said, and when I leaned in for the hug, I barely recognised the voice speaking to me. He sounded old, worn out, and above all, deflated.

"I've missed you so much," I whispered to him as we risked getting yelled at for an extended hug, but I didn't care, and I don't think Ollie did either. Human contact is one thing we crave, especially from those closest to us.

When we eventually parted again, each of us sat on opposite sides of the table, and I tried my best to hide the shock, but I did a lousy job. Ollie saw my reaction immediately and, not one to hide from it, he grinned at me.

"Not the picture of perfection you remember, huh?" he said with an extra wide grin that showed several blackened teeth. I tried to smile back at him, but inside, I grimaced.

"You'll always be beautiful to me," I said, and looked around the room. "Lively place. How are they treating you?"

"Same as anywhere else, I guess," he said. "Should be getting out of here tomorrow or the next day. Shipping me out to somewhere else, but they keep changing their mind. Guess I'm still one of those problem children."

Despite everything going on in his life, my friend still hung onto the one quality that most of his friends appreciated…his humour. He mightn't have told the funniest jokes or the most appropriate, but the positive thing is that he told them. He didn't let things get him down, or at least not in front of his friends. He cared too much about them to burden their lives with his struggles.

"They'll find you a new home soon," I said. "And then you'll have a chance to heal."

"I don't think I could ever heal, Em," he said, and when I heard those words, it just about broke my heart.

"Don't say that," I said, trying hard not to sound annoyed but still conveying enough support. "You deserve to heal just as much as anybody else."

"Yeah, maybe," he said.

I wanted to hug him again, to stand up, walk to his side of the table and just sweep him up into my arms. I could see the pressure he was under, the stress eating away at him. I saw my friend struggling beneath the constant weight of bad memories, his past never far from his mind. If I had the means at that very moment, I think I would have helped him escape, even if it meant picking up a gun and shooting those officers employed to watch him. I wanted to save my friend and felt completely powerless to do so. All I could do was sit there and watch his withered body fidget its way through an hour of unwanted attention from someone he deeply cared about. My presence only elevated his anxiety, and I knew that once he got back to his cell after leaving me behind, he would do everything in his power to try to forget.

All I could do was sit there and try my hardest to offer him a distraction, even if it was only a temporary one. As you already know, time isn't the same on the inside of a jail as it is on the outside, and while I had a limited amount with him, I needed to make it count.

"I saw Jack yesterday," I said, figuring that changing the subject would help. "I'm thinking of maybe applying for a job at his work. What do you think?"

"Doing what?"

"Washing cars," I said with a shrug. "Worked the prison kitchen for a while, washing pots and pans. How different can it be?"

Ollie laughed at that, and I wasn't sure whether it was the comparison between prison pans and a car, or me trying to wash one. His laughter, even if limited, sounded like gold to me, the first genuine reaction I heard from him since we sat down.

"How about you? Any job ideas?"

"I've been working on my writing, actually," he said, surprising me.

"Writing?" I felt my head tilt ever so slightly with curiosity. "What have you been writing about?"

"A kid growing up in the system who ends up joining this international assassin."

"You're writing a book?"

I just about fell off my chair, and not because of the book idea, but rather that Ollie found something to distract him from everything else going on in his life.

"Wouldn't say it's a book *yet*, but I do hope to make it a whole novel at some point." He grinned and leaned slightly forward. "He even has a sidekick named Emma."

"A sidekick?" I tried to sound offended, but it didn't work. Ollie could see right through me, loving the admiration I had for him.

"She's a little more than a sidekick, I guess, but not the main character."

"The protagonist, you mean?"

"The what?" Ollie looked confused.

"That's what you call the main good character. The main bad character is called the *ant*agonist."

"Ah, whatever," Ollie said. "Protagonist, antagonist. I just have good guys and bad guys, and I'm enjoying the freedom to make them do whatever I want."

"Geez, give you a few months and you'll have book agents chasing you down," I said with glee. Ollie's cheeks began to warm up.

"More like a few years," he said, but I could see he was enjoying himself.

For those final few moments of our visit, it felt like the old days when we used to hang out in someone's bedroom and just talk about anything and everything. Sometimes, it's those unscripted conversations that feel the most genuine, the ones that seemed to flow from nowhere in particular and for a few short minutes of our day, Ollie and I got to experience a small moment of freedom. I only wish he could have carried that conversation with him back to his cell instead of the heartache which I knew he felt when it came time for me to go.

CHAPTER 25

I decided that the best way for me to get my life on some sort of normal track, now that I had a fresh opportunity to do so, was to get a job. I had time to think my options through during the long ride home, and once I got to the other end, I had written down several ideas on a scrap bit of paper. Jack's dealership was not one of them and for very good reason. The last thing I wanted was for some minor problem to affect our relationship.

Like sex, work was another one of those things that could make or break a friendship. It was another one of those lines that once crossed, opened the door to a myriad of possibilities and not all of them good. I had seen friendships collapse loads of times, and normally, between people you would have never guessed could fall apart. One minute, the best of friends and the next, sworn enemies.

No, if I were going to do this, then I would need to find something on my own, stand on my own two feet, so to speak. I pretty much had an open schedule to work with, so whatever opportunities I did find wouldn't be affected by my hectic social calendar. Wednesday evenings between seven and nine were virtually the only time I couldn't work due to my support group meetings, which I had to sign up for as part of my parole conditions. If I miss even a single session, I go straight back inside. At the time of signing, I considered it a fair trade, and I had no intention of breaking that agreement.

When I got back to my building, the first thing I noticed was the guard sitting behind that clear perspex window of his office, watching me with a wry little grin. He even licked his lips and not in a subtle way, perhaps believing that such a move would immediately make me run to him. I couldn't work out which part of him disgusted me more, the greasy hair hanging down each side of his face, or the way the buttons of his shirt looked to be at breaking point thanks to his sizable gut. Rather than react, I ignored him completely and walked on. I did hear him mumble something under his breath as I passed by the open door, but I couldn't make it out, so I didn't bother reacting to it. Some guys just had a certain way with women.

When I reached my floor, a couple of women stood near the landing and immediately turned their backs to me as they continued the drug deal. One of them snatched a wad of cash from the other while holding out the baggie before looking at me over her shoulder.

"Need some?"

"Nah, I'm good, thanks," I said, wondering how long it would be before I accepted her offer.

Once back in my flat, I closed the door and at first, just leaned back against it before suddenly feeling an overwhelming sense of grief. I have no idea where it came from, a wall of dread and sadness slamming into me like a polar blast. Tears began to fall almost immediately and I felt myself slowly sliding to the floor, using the door to slow my descent. Once seated, I pulled my knees in close to my chest, buried my face between them and just…just cried.

What runs through a person's mind during that kind of emotional breakdown? Was I crying for me, for Ollie? I couldn't get Ollie's face out of my mind, not during the long ride back on the train and not at that moment sitting in my quiet flat, wondering why the universe hated us so much. He didn't deserve to be sitting in prison any more than I did, and yet society will tell you that we are the ones who should be locked up for life. It felt like our appearance alone triggered some people, the Rag Brigade of British Society.

I did cry for Ollie. The visit hadn't followed my thinking at all, and despite the last part of it feeling a lot more positive, it wasn't enough to fade away the rest of it. I hated myself for not being able to help him and then I hated myself even more for having my own problems to deal with, problems that he, in turn, wanted to help *me* with. It felt like a vicious cycle, each of us needing to lean on the other while bringing extra baggage.

Someone shouted about needing a ride out in the hallway and I heard a door slam shut a few doors down from my own. Heavy footsteps followed and I quietened my crying while listening to them pass by right outside my door. A voice called back from right next to me, and it sounded close enough for me to reach out and touch the person. That was when a wave of loneliness descended over me.

Loneliness isn't really something that had bothered me much growing up but it was at that moment, while sitting in a building full of complete strangers, that I suddenly felt more alone than ever before. I closed my eyes again, wanting the tears to start falling again, but even they seemed to evade my needs. Imagine feeling so lonely that you hate the very tears inside you for not falling from your eyes. I wanted to scream, to throw my handbag at a mirror or a window and hear the glass breaking with a satisfying crash. I wanted to kick the walls, punch the door, anything to take away that soul-crushing feeling of loneliness.

"I need a job," I finally managed to whisper into the silence of the room, and that's when I pushed myself off the ground and promised myself that I would do something to help myself.

For the next three days, I must have criss-crossed Wandsworth a dozen times over chasing job prospects, managing just two interviews and one of those lasting less than two minutes. It felt like I couldn't get past that incessant feeling of being judged by people everywhere I went. It felt like the whole world was watching me, always expecting me to do something bad. I actually expected someone to point at me and yell *Rag Brigade alert* the way they used to back in school, and for the rest of those walking by to join in.

By four o'clock on the third day, I was walking by a Sainsbury's when I checked my pockets and stared at the last five quid in my hand. I was hungry, thirsty, and feeling more than a little deflated. Going home after another day of failure felt like a mission in itself and I couldn't face the prospect of going to sleep hungry again. I wanted to call Jack for help, and I know I could have, but something refused to let me. Something about admitting defeat felt so wrong to me. I knew that if I called him and let him feed me, which I knew he would, then that would ensure I never struggled to achieve anything again. It would feel like giving up on life itself and just handing my needs and responsibilities over to someone else.

Looking at the entrance to the supermarket, I decided to get myself a bottle of water, grab a seat on a bench, and wait a couple of hours until a few of the takeaway shops got busy. People were always more willing to hire when they were under the pump and I figured I'd try my luck with a new approach.

Whether because of my depressive state or just because of feeling alone, I barely met anyone's eyes when I walked into the supermarket, keeping my own gaze down on the ground before me. I headed straight to the drinks, grabbed a bottle of water, a Snickers bar and headed for the register. My fingers felt jittery from the lack of food and while I know it wasn't the smartest option given I was in the middle of a supermarket, it was the fastest thing I could find and I wanted to get out of there in the shortest amount of time. All I had to do was get past the cash register and I could go back out into the late afternoon misery of the day.

"Emma?"

The voice sounded so surprised that I looked up for the first time since joining the back of the queue. The woman ahead of me finally pushed her trolley through the walkway and began fumbling through her purse when the cashier noticed me standing there, a cashier with a familiar face. It took me a moment to recognise the face, one I hadn't seen in a very long time. I knew that I should have known the girl, but not remembering from where made it harder to place her. The mole on the right side of her mouth should have been the clue, but I missed it the first time I looked at her. It was only when she briefly turned back to the lady to accept the cash that I gave her a proper look over.

"Jody, hey," I finally said as she swiped my goods across the scanner.

Jody Doyle once shared a bunk bed with me back at St. Agnes, her on the lower one. We weren't exactly best friends, but we respected each other enough not to step on each other's toes. We both had different people we hung out with, of course, especially me, who preferred the company of myself, but she was one of the few who never teased me for doing so. Jody was also one of the girls who stepped in to help defend some of the weaker girls from Lydia Nutworth.

"Hey, yourself," Jody said with the biggest grin on her face.

She looked good, healthy. Her long black hair shone as if covered in glass, her skin free from any hint of acne. When she smiled, her perfectly white teeth reminded me of Casey and a new sense of heaviness descended on me. "I haven't seen you in years. What have you been up to?"

"Not much," I said as I held out the fiver. Jody took it and waited for the cash drawer to pop open. I don't know why I said what I said next, the words almost rolling out of me before I had a chance to commit to them fully. Usually, I would have remained quiet, given that the woman standing behind me looked ready to tell Jody off for taking so long, but I said it anyway. "I'm actually looking for work."

Jody paused while counting out my change and looked at me wide-eyed, that same sweet grin of hers showing those perfect teeth a second time.

"Get out, are you serious?" She looked past me and called out to someone, completely ignoring the woman behind me, who was groaning loudly. "Hey, Rach, can you cover me for a minute?"

"Sure," the girl said, and Jody immediately backed away from the register as her friend arrived.

"Come with me," Jody said to me and didn't wait for an answer. When I didn't walk fast enough, she grabbed my hand and just about pulled me past all the other checkout registers towards the service desk. "Where's Donna?" Jody asked another girl behind the desk as she served a customer.

"On her break," the girl said without looking over, continuing to count out the change. "And two makes ten."

"Let's go," Jody told me and again began dragging me along the back of the registers.

"Where are we going?" I asked, still unsure of what I had walked into.

"To get you a job, silly," Jody said without looking back, and that was when I felt like the universe had finally sat up and taken notice.

Less than twenty minutes later, I walked out of the supermarket with a guaranteed job commencing the very next day. From what had been nothing more than an impulsive urge for a drink turned into a life-changing moment, one that I didn't immediately recognise. Jody had not only found me a job in a heartbeat, but she had also given me back my confidence, and that in itself gave me purpose. Hope is sometimes found in the most unlikely of places and at times when we least expect it, and that afternoon, it proved it to me yet again. What I didn't know was that fate still hadn't finished toying with me. It had another surprise waiting for me, and this time, it wouldn't let me go with a slap on the wrist.

CHAPTER 26

I once heard someone say that fate happens because of the choices we make along the way, each one leading us down a predetermined path with multiple forks that offer us various destinations. Whether I believe in it is another thing, but I do know that if I hadn't thrown away some of the choices I once had, then maybe I could have ended up in a far better situation than the one I eventually found myself in.

The job at Sainsbury's turned out to be more than just a blessing in disguise. When I began the following morning, it felt like a new beginning for me, and it didn't take long for me to forget all of those previous worries of mine. I met new people, made some friends, and overcame my anxiety in a very short amount of time. Some of the customers began to recognise me and would send me smiles and waves each time they came in for their groceries.

I had a couple of training days to begin with, of course, but I eventually found two duties I absolutely loved. The first was stacking shelves, replenishing items out on the main floor by unloading boxes and restocking depleted displays. It offered me a chance to hang out with other staff members and we would spend the time talking about all of the important things in life, like what plans we had on weekends, what sales were currently going on for clothes, and of course, boys.

The second duty I absolutely loved was working the cash registers. There's something special about interacting with customers on a more direct level and having a chance to make them smile. I often chatted to the regulars and always offered up compliments, regardless of how miserable they appeared. Sometimes, I could even turn a frown into a smile just by saying hello and commenting about the beautiful day outside, even though it was raining. Not everybody saw the humour, of course, and some people refused to answer me at all, but I didn't let that affect me. To me, it wasn't about them at all, but about me.

I often worked alongside Jody as well, and while I did appreciate her getting me the job, she refused to let me thank her, saying that I just happened to walk in at just the right time. We often chatted during our breaks, and we even ended up with some of the same friends. Given how well we got on and the similar interests we had, it made me wonder why she and I were never close while at St. Agnes.

"Because you were a loner," that private voice inside my head would say, reminding me of my defence mechanism back then.

My circle of friends began to grow as well, and within a couple of weeks, I not only got myself a new phone but also managed to add no less than twenty-three personal contacts, all of whom I considered friends. We often caught up on weekends, although it depended on the work roster, of course. Saturday nights were usually reserved for partying, though, and we always ended up at Lasers, a club located just a block up from the supermarket. Lasers were where we really let our hair down, dancing the night away to a bunch of body-moving trance tracks.

I think those first four to five weeks must have gone by in the blink of an eye as I settled into a routine I couldn't have imagined for myself. I worked multiple shifts a week, made good money, and got to hang out with friends whenever I wanted. I caught up with Jack several times and visited Ollie once when Jody's brother took her for their monthly visit to see their father, the man in the same prison as my friend. I even offered to throw in some money for fuel, but Gavin refused, saying they were heading there regardless.

It did feel a little weird to be sitting in that visiting room opposite Ollie with a friend seated just two tables over, but after I introduced Ollie to both Gavin and Jody, I managed to settle down again. He looked better than the previous time I had seen him and I think he had put on a bit of extra weight. His face still looked gaunt but nowhere near as bad. Ollie even smiled a lot more and made a few funny comments, trying to make me laugh the way he used to when he was a kid.

When I walked out of the prison after that visit, I didn't feel anywhere near as bad as I did the previous time. Ollie not only looked healthy, but he sounded so much happier, and even had added several chapters to his book. That alone told me he saw himself pursuing something once he got out again, and that in itself gave me hope that he was on the right track.

We drove mostly in silence during the return journey on account of the argument between Gavin and his father. While I didn't see Jody get involved, it was apparent she hadn't sided on her brother's side, and that meant for an uncomfortable ride home. She did wish me a good night once they dropped me off in front of my building, but I can tell you, it felt quite relieving to step out of the tension.

I didn't hear from her again until the next morning, when she texted me an apology for the way the trip ended up. I told her not to be silly and that I was grateful for the ride, and when she sent me back an emoji with its finger held to the side of its mouth as if thinking, I assured her I was fine. Her follow-up text showed that she believed me.

Good, then you'll come to the party tonight?

Have you ever found yourself at a mental crossroad, so sure that you wanted to go one way but something inside you told you not to? I had felt a similar way to the way I felt when Heather asked me to go with her to the cinema that long-ago night. It's like having a choice but with one option that feels just plain wrong. I had been to one of Jody's parties before, and it turned out great, which was why I couldn't understand why I was feeling apprehensive.

Too much information, I know, but I thought it might have been because I had only just started my period earlier that morning, and I don't know about you, but I like to plan for unforeseen moments of uncomfortable cramps and general tiredness. I usually felt weak during the heaviest days, almost lightheaded at times, and rarely did anything crazy like go to parties. The back pain alone was enough to keep me off my feet. This time, however, I didn't want to look like I was avoiding her and actually felt like mixing it up with people.

The thing about Jody's parties that I enjoyed the most was the sheer number of people a person could get lost with. Nearly all of our friends from the supermarket were there, plus a load more from Gavin's work. It wasn't all about the loud music and alcohol, either, with most people usually finding a place on the grass outside and just sitting around in small groups talking about anything that came to mind. Someone would always start a fire, and it was there I preferred to sit, pretending to be at some unknown campsite and spending the weekend out in the wilderness. I had never been camping before, so sitting around a fire was about the closest I had ever been to the experience.

I arrived at Jody's house around eight, and found the place already rocking with more than three or four dozen people spread throughout the home. I did force myself to eat half a pizza before I came though, just to make sure I had food in my stomach. While I had been getting better with the drugs and going for longer periods between hits, I wasn't so sure about avoiding alcohol, since it had a way of numbing the icky feelings associated with my time of the month. Call it a trade-off, if you will.

I know I haven't mentioned my habit for a while, and the truth is, I was battling my way through each day at a time. The first couple of meetings with the support group went really well and it actually felt like a victory each time I got to celebrate another clean week with fellow addicts. We cheered each other on and always offered support to those who caved during the week.

"Every day is a chance to start again," was what our counsellor would tell us each time we met, and for me, those words rang true.

When it came to the parties, I found that I could often trade one vice off against the other. Knowing how much more destructive heroin was for me, I found alcohol to be the lesser of the two evils and so generally gave in when someone offered me a drink. I could handle my liquor a lot easier, and so found myself able to enjoy the parties a lot more. Who knew it would be a decision that would cost me more than I ever expected?

The fight, when it finally started just before midnight, happened so quickly that most of the people hardly noticed it at all. Jody and Petra had continued their bickering from the previous day when they both got dragged into the manager's office over some missing money from one of the registers. Both girls had worked it and with neither balancing the till between their shifts, nobody knew when the error took place. The cameras had conveniently been down for maintenance, which left both of the employees in the firing line.

Jody insisted it must have been Petra on account of her register being short the previous week as well, but Petra pleaded her innocence, insisting that it must have been during Jody's spell on there when she relieved Petra for lunch. The manager gave them both a warning with a promise to watch them carefully.

The argument consisted of a single verbal exchange followed by a single slap, Petra's hand connecting with Jody's face like a gunshot. The crowd shrieked in shock, some people called for a fight, while others pulled the two girls apart. I was sitting in the kitchen talking with Clare when Petra stormed through, and when Jody came screaming into the room, I almost fell out of my chair from the surprise.

Clare and I took Jody to the bathroom, where we settled her down and wiped her face. The tears, brought on by the pain of a slap to the eyeball, had left long thin lines of mascara running down her face, and it took us a few minutes to fix her up again.

When we finished, Clare and Jody left before me while I attended to my own make-up situation. They left the door open, which was why I could hear Jody exclaim how she was going to sort Petra out the next time she saw her.

When the door suddenly closed, I looked over to see Gavin standing before me. The charming smile and adoring eyes I had often found attractive were gone, replaced by a look of hunger and lust. I could tell he was drunk, which was why it didn't immediately worry me. I smiled and continued applying lipstick.

"I'll be out of here in a sec," I said, trying to sound casual, but instead of opening the door again to let me out, Gavin walked towards me.

"Why the hurry?" he said, his voice low and almost condescending in nature. I tried to ignore the words but as I turned to leave, he grabbed me by the arm and tried to twist it around my back.

"Gavin, what the hell?" I said and winced as my shoulder felt ready to pop out of its socket. When he pulled it further around, I screamed, but he clasped a hand over my mouth hard enough to split my lip. That exquisitely thin band of pain was where my panic grew from. I tried to scream again, but his hand pressed harder over my face as his other grabbed a handful of hair. He pulled my head back, let go of my mouth and punched me hard in the stomach.

It felt like all the oxygen had been pushed out of my body as I desperately tried to suck air into my lungs. Gavin punched me a second time, swept my feet out from under me and followed me down as I crashed to the floor. Unable to scream and with the panic of suffocating to death debilitating me completely, I never felt him tear the top of my jeans, ripping the button and zipper apart and then pulling them down. It was only when I felt phantom fingers inside my panties that the realisation suddenly hit me.

My body went into a state of panicked revolt, my arms and legs fighting back as much as they could while I finally managed to push out a half-hearted scream. Gavin didn't have enough hands to control every part of me, but as it turned out, he didn't need to.

"Don't," he said after pushing himself up a bit, and the horror truly gripped me as I stared into the barrel of a pistol. One of his hands had wrapped itself around my throat, and I froze in an instant, the dark reality sinking in.

Gavin raped me, not once, but twice. I can't say it any blunter than that. He either didn't notice the blood or simply ignored it. When the first time wasn't enough for him, he made me get up while he cleaned himself off, forced me to dress myself again, and then walked me across the hallway to his bedroom while keeping the gun trained on me. With no worries of being interrupted and with the door locked, he took his time, only commenting on the blood when he finished that second time.

"If I had known, I would have waited," he said calmly while wiping himself with his t-shirt. He threw it at me as I lay motionless on the bed, too frightened to move. "Maybe we can do this again sometime," was the last thing he said to me just before he left the room.

I didn't hesitate to get out of not only the room but also the house. Don't ask me what time I ended up walking down the sidewalk, because I have no idea. Time wasn't exactly a priority to me at that point. All I wanted to do was get home. My neck hurt from where he grabbed me, my back hurt from where we fell to the floor, my ribs ached from him punching me, but I can tell you with the clearest of memories that nothing felt more disgusting than that feeling of him inside me. I walked with tears streaming down my face, unable to think logically until I remembered the phone in my pocket, and I called a taxi.

Half an hour after getting myself off that bed, I finally walked into my own flat, immediately locked the door and ran for the shower. I couldn't even bring myself to strip at first, just this overpowering urge to get into the shower pushing me on. Once I felt the water running down the inside of my shirt, I slowly collapsed to the shower basin and let the stream run over me, each drop trying its hardest to cleanse that disgusting feeling of abuse from my body. I couldn't scream, couldn't cry, just an overwhelming sense of violation blocking everything else.

I can't describe how I felt at that moment because it's not just one emotion, but many. I was relieved that I managed to make it home again and felt lucky not to have been killed like so many women caught in the same situation. I felt betrayed by someone whom I should have been able to trust, dirty for him treating me like nothing more than a piece of meat. I felt disgusted for seeing my blood on his thing, with some of it running down his leg as he stood before me.

If someone were to ask me how I managed to get over it, I don't think I ever did. The biggest mistake I made was not reporting it, like I should have, but the truth is, my not reporting it had nothing to do with Gavin, but everything to do with his sister. I had tasted loneliness, and I couldn't imagine what would have happened between Jody and me if I had made allegations against her younger brother. While they did argue like most siblings did, I knew that she loved and cared about him. Reporting him meant risking not only my friendship with her, but my entire way of life.

CHAPTER 27

I think I carried the secret of the rape around with me for almost three months before I finally lost the fight, and when that day came, it brought with it a whole new set of problems. I personally know of two other women who went through almost the same thing as me and didn't report their attackers, and both of them ended up falling victim to a lot more than a man's unwelcome lust. One became an alcoholic and died in a car crash a couple of years after her attack, while another turned to drugs and eventually got clean after spending years at the very bottom of society.

So how did I deal with it? I didn't, not at all. I only saw Gavin once after the attack when he came to pick Jody up from work one day. He saw me walking out of the supermarket ahead of his sister and immediately looked away with shame when our eyes met. I remember feeling this incredible urge to run up to him and spit in his face, to yell out what he had done to me and not care about who heard. I wanted them to know the pain and trauma he caused me; I wanted the world to understand that he wasn't the innocent nineteen-year-old everybody assumed him to be.

I didn't, of course, and I merely knocked back the ride Jody offered me and instead headed to the nearest bus stop. We also grew further and further apart, with her invitations to her parties eventually stopping altogether. I never told her why I didn't want to come over, with me always giving her some random excuse, like me having a headache, or cramps, or just not feeling well.

Do you know what hurts the most? It's that I couldn't even bring myself to telling Jack what happened, despite the chance to share coming up several times. It honestly felt like the more I hurt and suffered, the more I tried to protect those I cared about, Jody included. I wanted to save her the pain of knowing what actually happened and then losing her brother over it. I tried to save Jack the pain of knowing and then risking him going over there and confronting Gavin. What if Gavin shoots Jack, or Jack ends up hurting Gavin and then ends up in prison himself?

It's so easy for people to sit in judgment reading this, but the truth is, you will never understand what this felt like unless you go through the same thing with the same set of circumstances. Sometimes, it's much easier to speak harsh words about needing justice when justice may not be the answer for everything. Sometimes, it's much safer to let sleeping dogs lie.

My depression came back with a vengeance, and with it, my habit. I needed a hit almost the second I woke up, just to be able to cope with the day, and when the money from the job no longer covered my habitual needs, I began looking for other ways to make it. With Jody and me no longer talking at all, the supermarket began to feel more like a hindrance than anything, and when I ended up back prostituting to raise more funds, I found that the legal salary only served to keep me from making real money. I could make in just two tricks what it took me to earn in an entire day at the supermarket, so you do the maths.

Two weeks after the attack, I was back on the streets working a job I understood and earning serious money. The problem with earning serious money? It only increased my taste for heroin, and so the cycle began once more, with me needing to work more and more to fund the habit. I barely remember some days, going to bed with one stranger and waking up next to another, and all the while injecting myself multiple times a day just to feel alive.

You know that sometimes, regardless of how much alcohol or drugs are in your system, you just know when things are going to shit, and I could feel myself quickly imploding, not just physically, or financially, but mentally. My life was beginning to spiral out of control seriously, and I knew there was just one way out for me. I sometimes thought about how it would eventually end, either from an overdose, or murdered by some stranger in my bed who I didn't know or care about. It wasn't as if there were many options coming my way, and sometimes it's just easier to let the flow sweep you away.

The thing is, I didn't want to die, and I knew that if I kept going, that was precisely what was going to happen. I would die, from either the one way I mentioned, or the other. I felt like someone caught in a flooded river, unable to reach the banks and simply letting the current drag me along. Sometimes, the answers can be found in the most unlikely of places, and mine came to me in the middle of one of my support group meetings, given to me by someone I had never spoken with before.

I don't know why I went to the meeting that particular week, but I think I just wanted to see whether there was anything left to salvage of myself. I couldn't miss them anyway, since that meant a guaranteed return to prison. The meeting had only just started when a girl walked in, sat down, and immediately got up to leave again. She looked new and out of place, and when our counsellor called her back, the girl flipped her off.

"You don't attend, you lose your parole," the counsellor called to her, and that was when the girl yelled something back that immediately pricked my ears.

"So? Maybe I'd *rather* be back inside," was what she said before storming out.

That was the moment it hit me, a realisation, of sorts. What do people call those types of moments, sometimes? An epiphany? Whatever it is, something about her words woke me up in a way that refused to fade away again. I think it might have been like someone throwing an overboard victim on a cruise ship, a life ring. I caught it fairly easily, but the real question was what I was going to do with it.

It wasn't until the following week, while standing in front of the door leading into the hall, that I finally admitted the truth to myself, that if I continued down the path of destruction, then I may as well just end it myself on the spot. Again, I didn't want to die, so I knew that wasn't going to be an option for me. Instead, I turned away from the next potential meeting and never went back. Three weeks later, the police came and arrested me, and by the following afternoon, I found myself sitting inside a prison cell surrounded by eighty other women in B-Unit.

In less than a month, I had gone from working at a supermarket and enjoying life to hating the very air I breathed and feeling closer to death than at any point during my entire life. I felt deflated, lacking any sort of will to live, and yet still refused to give up. I wanted to fight for my life, and yet couldn't work out what life I kept believing I could have. In a way, I felt like I had some sort of imposter syndrome, as if I wasn't supposed to be out in the world like everybody else. It wasn't until years later that I discovered that a lot of the kids who went through the system like me felt exactly the same way.

Imagine spending every moment of your waking life surrounded by people who didn't consider your existence as being worthy of life itself, people who went out of their way to keep you as miserable as possible. And then, to make matters worse, you had people in the system who made themselves feel better by causing yet more misery through relentless bullying and intimidation.

Once I was back in prison, I initially felt like I had somehow betrayed myself. Why the hell would I go out of my way to get myself thrown back inside when I spent so many months and years dreaming of the day when I could finally walk out. Some people call it self-sabotage, and the first meeting I had was three days after my arrival, where I was explained how a lot of those who had been institutionalised would go about ensuring they would end up right back inside.

Was I really institutionalised? I didn't think so, but I couldn't be sure during those first few days. The counsellor who came to the jail every other day to meet with severe cases kept telling me that depression caused horrific side effects, one of which was to keep oneself in a place where they had no need for personal responsibility. They were telling me that I came back to prison because I wanted to scrounge off the same system I had been a part of since being a baby.

"You're used to it," the woman told me in front of about ten others. "You're used to it, and it's just easier for you to go back to what you understand."

She made it sound dirty, made me sound like a societal leech, if you will. I felt embarrassed by her words, and I could see others trying to avoid eye contact with her for fear of getting singled out as well. Yes, granted, I had been a part of the system for a long time, but that didn't mean that I deserved to live any less than she did. I just didn't have the same opportunities as most people, and I had made some bad decisions on top of that, which, let's face it, are the first thing most people tend to focus on.

I think I must have walked around the unit like a zombie that first week, unsure of whether the nightmare had been on the outside or the inside. I couldn't work out who I was anymore, and whenever I looked in the mirror, I saw a stranger's face staring back at me, a stranger who wore the scars of a life lived in hell.

The first cellmate I had when I arrived in the unit was a fairly new inmate herself, serving her first week of a two-year stretch for assaulting a police officer. She tried to ask me a lot of questions, but I often pretended to be asleep and avoided conversation as best I could. She seemed like such a sweet girl, and I felt bad for ignoring her, but the voices in my head just happened to be screaming a lot louder than hers.

I don't think I really broke through that shell until a couple of weeks later, when Jack finally managed to track me down. It wasn't just the attack that stopped me from contacting him. It might have also had a bit to do with losing face. I felt embarrassed that I couldn't truly open up to him the way he would have expected of me. We had promised each other to always be open, all three of us, and yet I felt unable to, given how the situation would appear from someone else's viewpoint. Looking in from the outside, this was just another junkie making excuses for her troubles, or maybe a junkie wanting to hide away from he truth.

You have no idea how hard it was for me to sit opposite my friend and lie to his face, answering almost every question of his with some pre-rehearsed response. No, I haven't been avoiding you, and yes, everything *is* fine with us. Every answer I gave him tasted like rust on my tongue, each lie rolling out after the previous. I saw him try to smile throughout the visit while doing his best to shield the real feelings within. I wanted so badly to tell him about the attack, but with me unable to watch him afterwards, I knew he would go and confront Gavin, and that meant a guaranteed confrontation as well. I couldn't risk it.

When I finally gave Jack a final hug and watched him head for the door, I honestly thought I would never see him again. Why would he want to hang around someone who so blatantly lied to his face, and a junkie at that? I believed in my heart that I had wronged him for the last time and that visit would be our last. I could feel such a sense of dread in my soul that I returned to my cell in much the same state as when I first arrived at the prison.

It's funny how you can look at some people and think you can predict their future for them. Take a junkie, for example. There's always that distinctive look of deceit hanging about them, a kind of natural warning sign for others to beware and hang onto their purses and wallets. You expect them to commit crimes, expect them to end up in jail, and once there, treat the front gate like a kind of revolving door. They never want to heal themselves, but rather keep living a life of endless highs paid for by unwary victims of crime.

I sometimes wonder whether other inmates see us the same,

expecting us to screw up at some point and get sent right back to where we belong. Maybe that's why Maddie knew I would be back, another junkie just following the same predictable routine as the rest of them. Maybe that was why she waited to get me for her losing Tash, an attack she somehow blamed me for.

When the attack on me came, I barely saw it coming, thanks to my depressed state after visiting with Jack. I walked back into my cell wanting nothing more than to slip under the blanket of the bottom bunk, turn to face the wall, close my eyes, and drift off into that void between being awake and asleep.

"Maddie says hi," a voice spoke before I felt three sudden jolts, each one caused by something hitting me in the back. I didn't have time to see who had hit me, the world suddenly a spiral of haze and confusion as the ground came up to meet me and just before I hit the floor, I wondered if this was how it finally ended.

CHAPTER 28

I languished in a coma for more than four days after getting stabbed in the back three times, with one of those thrusts piercing a kidney that I subsequently lost. The most damage came from nobody finding me for almost ten minutes as I lay in my cell, bleeding out, the rest of the unit down on the ground floor watching a film on the unit television.

Maddie had taken great care to time her attack. I only found out through sources in later years that she actually had a friend staying just three doors up from me at Logan House. She could have had me killed at any time, but that wasn't her style. She enjoyed watching the hit, loved seeing the blood and the pain of her hatred. When she paid for someone to die, she paid for the show itself, not to hear about it from someone else. They say she came into my cell not long after the stabbing and kneeled right down beside me, close enough to smell the blood, but I can't confirm that. Lucky for me, I passed out moments after the attack and woke up days later.

I found out who had carried out the attack from Sue, who had been working inside the medical wing as one of the billets. It was while mopping the floor in my room that she told me. According to her, Reggie had been hanging around another girl close to Maddie, and our old friend eventually ended up as one of Maddie's little toys. She used her for more than just stabbings, and I wasn't the first Maddie had sent Reggie to take care of.

Now that I had effectively been flagged as vulnerable, the system transferred me into a protection unit at a different jail entirely, one where the least desirable people in the system lived. We're talking about the kind of people even criminals don't want to associate with, like sex offenders, convicted law enforcement officials, and rats, the type of inmates who talk to officers. And once again, the little black sheep of the world ended up in a place I didn't belong, where I didn't fit in, and where I certainly didn't conform to the usual categories of inmates. I was an outsider again, the odd child, and destined to remain alone once more.

The others didn't see me as an outsider, of course. They just saw me as a new face and someone to bring a bit of change to their otherwise monotonous routine. I represented a difference, and that was why I got treated like a kind of celebrity for a few days, with every person in the unit wanting to introduce themselves to me. When it was apparent I wasn't going to get any alone time, not even in my cell, I headed out into the common area where several women encircled me before bombarding me with questions. What was I in for, why did I end up in F-Unit, and how long was my sentence?

I ended up spending the rest of my sentence in that unit, and the funny thing is, despite having the opportunity to apply for parole, I didn't. Instead, I remained behind bars and fought my demons every single day until they finally disappeared forever. My time with drugs was finished, and I knew that if I wanted to live a life, and I mean a *proper* life, then I needed to make an honest decision. I could no longer afford to let those demons run my life, or else they would steal my very soul.

When I finally walked out of HMS Holloway in the summer of 2009, I can honestly say that I felt like a completely different person. I felt clean, in a sense, or maybe cleansed is a better word for it. I felt like I had been stripped of most of those dark shadows living in my head, those horrific demons pushed out completely. It wasn't just my mind that felt rehabilitated. Wait, did I really just say that word? Rehabilitated. I think before that day, I never believed prison could ever rehabilitate someone, but I turned out to be the biggest truth bomb of all. I proved that it was possible, but only with the right attitude. That's the key, I guess, the person *wanting* to be rehabilitated.

It wasn't just my inner self that felt clean, but also my outside. My skin had healed itself over the previous year. All traces of my substance abuse vanished. My face cleared up, and my skin went from looking like a dull grey to healthy pink again. I felt like I had finally broken through the barriers...all except one.

I put my success down to one person, a woman named Myriam Fairchild. She started a new program about eight months after I arrived at Holloway, some new approach to helping addicts. They called it a prototype course or something, and only a select few were chosen. I volunteered because, at the time, I had suddenly decided to change my ways and ended up being chosen.

Myriam changed my way of thinking from the moment I met her. She knew things about me without me ever telling her. She could recognise my traits and my defence mechanisms to deal with them. I related to everything she spoke about, and when it came time to commit to change, I made it without a second thought.

The course wasn't only a group thing where we sat around in a circle telling each other stories about who we were and where we came from, although that was a big part of it. No, Myriam preferred to include one-on-one sessions, similar to a proper counsellor, which she was. I spent hours with her, the sessions spread out over eight months, and each one gave me something new that I could use.

It was during one of those one-on-one sessions that the subject of my mother came up, and I don't know how or why, but at some point, unbelievable grief flooded out of me. I'm talking relentless sobbing that just wouldn't quit, my hands trembling, my body shaking, and my insides twisting and turning under the immense grief. Myriam just sat there, a blank expression on her face as she let me deal with the grief in my own way.

When I walked out of Holloway some months later, I had been given a new lease on life thanks to her, but with one condition. She warned me that if I wanted to be whole again, and I mean completely whole, then I would need to confront the one demon I had been avoiding my entire life, and until I did so, I would risk constantly falling back into the shadows. That demon's name was Daniel Duffy.

If you had asked me about Duffy before that day, I think I would have broken down the same way I did when Myriam spoke about him during that constructive session. Just *thinking* about his name turned me into a mess. It was, after all, his doing that robbed me of so much, and while it can never be fully proven, I always believed that it was because of his actions that I ended up the way I did. His murdering my mum robbed me of the chance of ever having a relationship with her. In a way, he stole my life for whatever reason and left me to face the world alone.

I had to face my demon. That was how Myriam put it, anyway. I had to sit in front of the man and ask him all the questions I had buried deep inside me, the questions I had spent a lifetime trying to run from. Only when I faced the demon and asked my questions could I truly be free of the torment I had been carrying for the better part of twenty-five years.

When Jack picked me up from Holloway that day, he pulled up in a 1969 Mustang convertible, with the roof rolled down and the breeze blowing his long black hair around. He had on these old-school Ray-Bans that somehow made him look much more mature than he was, and I think I fell in love with my friend just a little bit more.

He climbed out of the driver's seat when he saw me walk through the gate, and after a hug I had been waiting weeks for, he opened the passenger side door and waved me inside. That drive home is something I can never forget. The wind in our hair and the sun on our faces made the world feel so much more real. I could smell freedom in the air, and not the kind I had breathed in the previous time I walked out of jail.

Jack insisted that I stay with him for the foreseeable future, and I can't begin to tell you how proud I was when he pulled into the driveway of his very own home. The kid who had once struggled to believe he would survive until adulthood had not only worked an incredible job, but he had also been approved for a home loan.

"It's beautiful," I told him once we climbed out of the car, and I seriously meant it.

That night, Jack sat down with me and showed me how to use the internet, something I hadn't ever taken an interest in. An hour later, I found the prison where the final demon of my life lived and remained behind bars for more than two decades. As it turned out, the man who had caused so much grief in my life lived just a few minutes' drive from a home I had been welcomed into when I was just four months old and lived in until I was seven.

I sent the email almost immediately, and the next day, I kept checking my inbox repeatedly, waiting for a response. When none came and with my patience virtually nonexistent, I decided to phone instead and spoke to this lovely lady who took care of everything. The thing is, Daniel Duffy didn't have to see me. He could have refused, and that would have been the end of my chance at freedom. I actually don't know why he agreed to see me at all, but he eventually did, with word coming through two days later. You can imagine the mixed emotions I felt at the news.

Belmarsh Prison sat on the eastern side of London, and Jack insisted on driving me there the very next day. Why so soon, you ask? Because I wasn't prepared to follow my old pattern of putting things off. I needed to face this demon head-on and as soon as possible if I was going to cleanse myself of the bullshit, finally. That's how Myriam put it, anyway. I texted her my intentions that very night, and I found her response waiting for me on my phone the next morning.

I expected to feel scared during that drive, but the truth is, I don't think I had ever felt more alive. I guess you could compare it to driving to a movie theatre to finally see that blockbuster you've been waiting months to see. I wanted to see him so bad that I had to get Jack to stop at three different places so that I could pee because of my nerves. I know it sounds weird, but it wasn't the seeing him part that I felt so excited about. It actually had nothing to do with confronting the killer of my mother. What I felt excited about was the prospect of finally being able to face life without those dreaded demons in my head. Myriam told me that I would feel the difference the moment I walked out of that meeting, and it was that moment I was looking forward to. Daniel Duffy just happened to be the barrier standing between me and that moment.

When I walked into the visitor's room, the officer didn't stop at the normal reception desk where I assumed I had to go. He continued on, passing by all of the tables and chairs until he reached a door at the far end. He knocked on it once, and a moment later, another guard opened it.

"Visitor for Duffy," the first guard said. The second one gave me an up-and-down look and waved me inside.

Unlike the main visiting area, this room was much smaller, with just a row of chairs placed in front of a wall made up of clear perspex panels, each one with several holes drilled into the middle. The sections were divided up into these little booths, with one inmate seated behind each panel. I could see four or five people already speaking with their respective prisoners, with some of them eyeballing me when I walked past.

"This way," the guard said and beckoned for me to follow. He led me to one of the empty booths and motioned for me to sit. "He'll be here shortly."

I sat down, feeling my insides tighten as if waiting for the executioner to come and end me. I guess, in a weird kind of way, that's exactly what he was to me, an executioner of sorts. My leg kept jittering up and down, the knee bouncing just high enough to hit the underside of the bench I tried hard not to lean on.

What I remember most during those few minutes of waiting was the overwhelming sense of purpose. I don't think I had ever gone into a prison to visit someone and felt like fate itself depended on the outcome the way this one did. Most visits were about catching up, about making sure a loved one is doing OK. The visits go by as if the people were sitting at home enjoying a cup of tea around the kitchen table. Not so this one.

This visit had nothing to do with making sure anybody was OK. It was to imitate a cup of tea around the kitchen table, or to show interest in whatever has been going on in each other's respective lives. This was about confessing to the truth, about making peace with God…or the devils.

When the moment arrived, the man who sat down looked nothing like the mug shot I had stared at countless times in the years I had known about him. In his photo, Duffy looked young, healthy, and almost handsome. Who knows where he might have ended up were it not for that little side trek of his? The man who sat down before me looked almost sixty, most of his blond hair long gone, save for a few strands around the outside of his skull. He'd put on weight and lots of it, the jowls almost hiding most of his earlier characteristics.

"You're Megan's little girl?" he asked. I nodded, my mouth suddenly feeling much too dry.

I honestly don't know what I expected to happen. Myriam had only told me so much, mostly to do with how such a meeting would affect my future. She focused more on the end result rather than the process of getting there. I guess I should have asked her for a list of questions I should be asking, kind of like a guide to help me, but I somehow knew that wasn't going to help me. This was *my* meeting, based on *my* experiences, a private moment for me to confront something almost impossible to comprehend.

"You look like her," Duffy said, his tone more matter-of-fact. I did note how he didn't look at me continuously, but rather sporadically, as if nervous to meet my gaze.

"Why?" I suddenly asked, the single-word question almost punching its way out of me as if summoned by someone else entirely. I felt the word hit the barrier between us and bounce off like an unwanted order. Duffy didn't flinch in the sense of him physically moving, but he did lower his eyes a lot further when he heard the word.

For a moment, we just sat there in silence, both of us a little unsure of what to make of the situation. I don't think he really knew what to expect of the meeting any more than I did, and so neither of us took charge. We just kind of sat there opposite each other and trying to feel our way through it.

"I know you came here looking for answers, kid," he finally said. Hearing him call me that word irritated me, and I wanted to tell him not to call me that, but then again, I knew it wouldn't help the situation. I didn't come here to hurt the man, nor yell at him. I hadn't come for the kind of confrontation you might be expecting, and I think he knew that. "The truth is, I've been looking for the same answers my entire life."

"What sort of life did you have?" I asked, suddenly curious.

"Not one that dissimilar to your own," he said. "I grew up in a home similar to St. Agnes." Hearing him mention the place sent chills through me, the goosebumps on my arms standing to attention. He must have seen my expression at hearing him mention it. "Yes, I know you spent time there. I also knew you spent time with that family in Bromley." More chills.

"You've been spying on me?"

"Not spying," he said. "Just curious, really. The guilt wasn't something I could ever run away from, and I guess I just wanted to see if you were doing OK."

"Why would you care about how I ended up?"

I started to feel my anger building and wondered whether that was part of the cleansing process. Myriam had told me about the possibility of a range of emotions sweeping over me during the confrontation, but not how to deal with them.

"I was an angry person back then, but as the years went by, I started seeing that this wasn't something I could blame anybody else for. The hatred I had for the way I was brought up. It fueled my anger and ensured I could never live a normal life. I felt guilty about making you a victim of that anger of mine."

"You're saying this all happened because you were angry?"

He looked embarrassed, his eyes constantly casting themselves down as he avoided my gaze again.

"Hatred has a way of giving a person the fuel needed to self-sabotage their existence. It will drive a person almost mad to do things that they can use as an excuse." He smiled, but the expression lacked any hint of warmth, rather giving him the irony he wanted to convey. "I always blamed everybody else for my problems, wanting them to take responsibility for screwing things up for me. It's strange how my own anger was what eventually led me here, a place where I could finally realise that we're all given the same power to determine our own lives. All I had to do was come to terms with a past I couldn't change, accept it as history, and move on."

When I heard him mention the words self-sabotage, something inside me clicked, like a key unlocking some ancient rusty chest. I suddenly felt like I was looking into a mirror and seeing myself in another dimension. His hatred, his anger, his self-sabotage sounded almost exactly like my own. I had always used them as an excuse, not to anybody else, but rather to myself. That was how I made it OK to use drugs, to not stick with a proper job, to take shortcuts. I would tell myself that it was who I was because of my background.

I could have stayed there and asked more questions, but the moment I heard him speak those words, I realised I no longer needed to listen to him. You might have expected me to forgive him, like I've always been told. Isn't that what cleanses a person? When they forgive those who wronged them? I call bullshit on that. Why would I forgive a man who murdered my mum and left me alone to fight my way through this world?

I heard him call out to me as I walked away, but I didn't turn back. As far as I was concerned, Daniel Duffy disappeared into the past the moment he made me realise that the only person I needed to heal myself from was me, and I had done that by setting myself free. I didn't forgive him; I forgave myself, and sometimes, just forgiving yourself is enough to move on.

I managed to walk out of that prison feeling like I had found what I came looking for. Myriam had given me the directions on how to get here, and Daniel Duffy gave me the key to unlock the chest I had been carrying around inside me this entire time. When I reached the car park and saw Jack waiting for me, I knew where my real future lay, just as it always had, with the best friends a girl could ever ask for.

CHAPTER 29

Now that you have read Emma's tale, I hope you're prepared for the final chapter in our story, because the hardest one is yet to come. Before we go there, however, I want you to know that I did eventually find out about what Gavin Doyle did to Emma, and I can promise you that he didn't get away with it. After convincing Emma that she needed to report him, my closest friend finally agreed to let me drive her to the local police station, where she made an official statement.

The investigation lasted less than two days, with Gavin breaking down when confronted by authorities. He ended up pleading guilty to two counts of rape and two counts of assault and served nine years. When Emma and I left the courtroom on the day he was sentenced, a woman approached us and embraced Emma at length. Jody never knew what her brother had done, and to her credit, she never doubted Emma's story either. They didn't rekindle their friendship, however, with Emma choosing to leave that chapter of her life behind.

The one thing Emma continued to do for years, however, was regular counselling sessions with Myriam. She even brought me in on one of them, and after spending the hour with her, I ended up signing up for my own sessions. Emma was right about her. She really did know her way around a person's mind, and even predicted several of the reasons behind my own anxieties.

The reason Emma brought me into the sessions at all was so she could share a dark secret that she had been holding back from both me and Ollie, and for good reason. She tried to kill herself, not once, but twice, both times failing. She told me that she tried to do so to protect us, to save us from needing to deal with a junkie's lies. I can promise you that not a dry eye ended up in the room that day, as some very uncomfortable truths came out, and not only from her.

I do want to share one final little detail about Emma's story that I know she didn't touch on, and I think it's one that's quite important to bring up, considering the story you've just read. It's something she shared with me a couple of years after she met with Daniel Duffy and about six months before she finally shared the whole Gavin Doyle thing. I don't blame her for wanting to keep that other relationship with Ollie to herself, even through the writing and conversations we had about this book, but she did eventually find the strength to share it all.

While it wasn't always clear to me, I did have my suspicions, and Emma finally confirmed them when she told me the truth about her and Ollie during a particularly nasty snowstorm in the Winter of 2017. Their relationship was a lot closer than she may have led us to believe, me included, and it was because of what happened in the subsequent years that she didn't want to go there.

The first time she ever had feelings for Ollie was during that whole summer trip to Bexhall. During her confession to me, she said that she first noticed her feelings that time when Ollie came charging past us right before he ended up running into the ocean fully clothed. You remember that part, don't you? We all ended up jumping into the water together and standing in a circle while holding hands.

It was during those weeks in that seaside village that their fondness for each other grew, a couple of young teens trying to work out where they belonged in the world. I didn't know it at the time, but there was a moment during the late-night Monopoly games when I went to the bathroom and they…kissed for the very first time. We're not talking a huge tongue-in-mouth pash here, just a quick peck on the lips to test the waters.

As our friendship grew over the years, so did their relationship, which wasn't always platonic. They may not have gotten right down to the sex part with each other, but they did explore things in other ways. This isn't about that side of things anyway. I think we can both agree that Emma's sex life is something best left in the past now that she has opened up about the darker part of it. I'd like to respect her wishes and keep it to the basics.

The reason I'm telling you all this is because you're going to need it in order to understand the next chapter of our story, the part where Ollie takes centre stage. His is a story that doesn't come easy, and I've had to step in a few times to help him write it. I guess you could call him the bad boy of our group, the one who didn't always take the high road when it came to navigating the rocky journey through the system.

Ollie's story begins in a very similar way to my own, with his mother caught up in that never-ending cycle of drugs and over-doses. Unlike Emma and me, however, he didn't immediately end up in the system, due to having family willing to look after him. The irony is that the family he had to care for him ended up being the very same family that caused so many of the issues Ollie would face later in life.

It's probably best if you hear it from the man instead, and so, I will hand you over to him now. He's written the following story for you, which I know will answer most of the questions you should have at this point. I must warn you, however, as it's far from easy reading, as so much to do with the system rarely is. Just be ready to shed some tears, because if my reaction to reading it is anything to go by, you're going to shed a few.

Thank you so much for reading Hidden Paths, and I hope you're ready for the final chapter in this series, with Resilient Paths set for release in February 2026. In the meantime, would you be so kind as to leave a review for this book? It does mean a great deal to me and will ensure others will also experience this series. Thank you.